Sophie
Gets Real

Other books in the growing Faithgirlz!™ library

The Faithgirlz!™ Bible
NIV Faithgirlz!™ Backpack Bible
My Faithgirlz!™ Journal

The Sophie Series

Sophie's World (Book One)
Sophie's Secret (Book Two)
Sophie Under Pressure (Book Three)
Sophie Steps Up (Book Four)
Sophie's First Dance (Book Five)
Sophie's Stormy Summer (Book Six)
Sophie's Friendship Fiasco (Book Seven)
Sophie and the New Girl (Book Eight)
Sophie Flakes Out (Book Nine)
Sophie Loves Jimmy (Book Ten)
Sophie's Drama (Book Eleven)

Nonfiction

No Boys Allowed: Devotions for Girls
Girlz Rock: Devotions for You
Chick Chat: More Devotions for Girls
Shine On, Girl!: Devotions to Make You Sparkle

Check out www.faithgirlz.com

SOPHIE
Gets Real

12

Previously titled Sophie's Encore

Nancy Rue

ZONDER**kidz**

ZONDERVAN.com/
AUTHORTRACKER
follow your favorite authors

ZONDERKIDZ

Sophie Gets Real
Previously titled *Sophie's Encore*
Copyright © 2006, 2009 by Nancy Rue

This is a work of fiction. The characters, incidents, and dialogue are products of author's imagination and are not to be construed as real. Any resemblance to actual events or persons, living or dead, is entirely coincidental.

Requests for information should be addressed to:

Zondervan, *Grand Rapids, Michigan 49530*

Library of Congress Cataloging-in-Publication Data

Rue, Nancy N.
    [Sophie's encore]
    Sophie gets real / Nancy Rue.
       p. cm. (Sophie series ; [bk. 12]) (Faithgirlz)
    Previously published in 2006 under the title, Sophie's encore.
    Summary: Although Sophie's faith is shaken after her baby sister is born with Down Syndrome and as she tries to help a troubled girl at her school, the other Corn Flakes and Dr. Peter are there to lend their support.
    ISBN 978-0-310-71845-1 (softcover)
    [1. Cliques (Sociology)—Fiction. 2. Down syndrome—Fiction. 3. People with mental disabilities—Fiction. 4. Schools—Fiction. 5. Christian life—Fiction. 6. Virginia—Fiction.]
    I. Title.
    PZ7.R88515Sjke 2006
    [Fic]—dc22
                                                       2009004602

Published in association with the literary agency of Alive Communications, Inc., 7680 Goddard Street, Suite 200, Colorado Springs, CO 80920. www.alivecommunucations.com

Zonderkidz is a trademark of Zondervan.

Interior art direction and design: Sarah Molegraaf
Cover illustrator: Steve James
Interior design and composition: Carlos Estrada and Sherri L. Hoffman

Printed in the United States of America

So we fix our eyes not on what is seen,
but on what is unseen.
For what is seen is temporary,
but what is unseen is eternal.

—2 Corinthians 4:18

One

Sophie. Yo — Sophie LaCroix!" Sophie looked up at her best friend Fiona and blinked behind her glasses.

Fiona pointed. "Are you putting both feet into one leg of your sweats for a reason?"

Sophie looked down at the bulging left side of her PE sweatpants. Fiona sat beside her on the locker-room bench, one magic-gray eye gleaming. The other one was hidden by the golden brown strand of hair that always fell over it.

"Are you thinking up a new character for a film?" Fiona said. "Yes! We haven't done a movie in so long that the whole Film Club's going into withdrawal."

Sophie shook her honey brown hair out of her face. "I wish that was what I was thinking about." She got untangled and pulled on her PE sweatpants. "I can't keep my mind off my mom."

"What's wrong with your mom?" Willoughby, another member of their group, bounded in and stopped in front of Sophie, brown curls springing in all directions. "Um, Soph? How come you have your sweats on backward?"

Sophie groaned and wriggled out of them again.

"Her mom's been in labor since early this morning," Fiona told Willoughby. "Sophie's a little freaked."

Willoughby's hazel eyes, always big to begin with, widened to Frisbee size. "Your mom's having your baby sister today? Why are you even here? Why aren't you at the hospital?"

"It could take all day, and it's not like Sophie could help deliver the baby," Fiona said. "She can't even get her clothes on right. Soph, your shirt's on inside out."

Sophie looked down at the fuzzy backward letters GMMS—for Great Marsh Middle School—and groaned again. "I'm not even gonna be able to change her diapers. I'll probably put them on her head or something."

"You put diapers on somebody's head?" At the end of the bench, Kitty's china-blue eyes went almost as round as Willoughby's.

Kitty was the fourth member of their six-girl group. She was just back from changing clothes in a restroom stall. Although she was finally sprouting spiky hair after her chemotherapy for leukemia, she still had a tiny hole in her chest. It let the doctors put in medicine and take out blood without sticking her every time. She always changed her shirt out of sight of the girls a few lockers down—the mostly rude ones Sophie and her friends secretly referred to as the "Corn Pops." Those girls decided what was cool. A hole in the middle of somebody's chest *wasn't*.

"What about diapers on her head?" Kitty asked again.

"She hasn't put Pampers on her little cranium so far," Fiona said. "But then, the baby's not born yet."

"Any minute now," Willoughby told Kitty. And then she let out one of her shrieks that always reminded Sophie of a hyper poodle yelping.

Kitty giggled and threw her arms around Sophie, just as Sophie pulled her T-shirt off over her head. A few tangled moments passed before Sophie could get it off her face and breathe again. By then, Darbie and Maggie, the final two, were there. Maggie shook her head, splashing her Cuban-dark bob against her cheeks.

"You can't wear your shirt for a hat," she said, words thudding out in their usual matter-of-fact blocks.

Maggie was the most somber of the group, but that was just Maggie. Although the lip-curling Corn Pops called them "Flakes"—which was where their very-secret name "Corn Flakes" came from—Sophie and her friends let each other be the unique selves they figured God made them to be.

Only at the moment, Sophie wasn't feeling unique. Just weird.

Darbie hooked her straight reddish hair behind her ears. "You're all in flitters, Sophie," she said.

Darbie still used her Irish expressions, even though she had been in the U.S. for more than a year. Sophie loved that, but she barely noticed now.

"Her mom's having her baby sister right this very minute," Willoughby told Darbie, with a poodle-shriek. "Our newest little Corn Fl—"

"Shhhh!" Maggie said.

Willoughby slapped her hand over her own mouth, and Sophie glanced down the row of lockers to make sure the Corn Pops hadn't heard. It didn't look like it.

Nobody outside the group knew about the Corn Flake name. Being a Corn Flake was a special thing, with a code that was all about behaving the way God wanted them to. The Corn Flakes had agreed a long time ago that they couldn't risk Julia and her group finding out and twisting it all up.

Still, it was hard not to talk about it, especially when it came to Sophie's soon-to-be-born sister. They had plans for making her the newest Corn Flake.

"Sophie's so nervous about the baby," Kitty said to Maggie, "she's about to put a diaper on her head."

"Of course she is," Julia Cummings said as she walked by. She was the leader of the three Corn Pops, who all rolled their eyes in agreement.

But that was all they did. The Corn Pops had gotten into so much trouble for bullying the Corn Flakes in the first six months of seventh grade, they didn't dare try anything they'd get caught at. Or, as Fiona put it, there would be "dire consequences." That was Fiona language for "big trouble."

And now that her Corn Flakes were all around her, helping her get her shoes on the right feet, Sophie didn't feel quite so much like the pieces of her world had been mixed up and put back together wrong. A new baby was big stuff, but Fiona, Willoughby, Kitty, Darbie, and Maggie could make even that easier.

As the Flakes hurried into the gym, a whistle blew and Sophie jumped.

"Does Coach Yates have to toot that thing so hard?" Willoughby said. "Doesn't she know Sophie's mom is having a baby?"

"I don't think so," Maggie said.

Coach Yates, their PE teacher with a graying ponytail so tight it stretched her eyes at the corners, gave the whistle another blast.

The Flakes skittered into line for roll call. In the next row, a way-skinny boy with a big, loose grin that filled up most of his face turned to Sophie. "So when's Film Club gonna do another film?" His voice cracked, as usual, bringing titters from Corn Pop Cassie in front of him.

"Not now, Vincent," Kitty said. "Her mom's having a baby."

"What's that got to do with it?" Vincent said.

"Boys," Willoughby whispered to Sophie. "They're so clueless."

Sophie nodded, but she really did wish she was deep in daydreams about a new and fabulous character for a Film Club movie the Corn Flakes could make with the Lucky Charms. That was the name the Flakes had secretly given to Vincent and his two friends, partly because they weren't absurd little creeps like *some* boys they knew.

"Is your mom okay?" Jimmy Wythe said. His eyes, as blue as a swimming pool, were soft.

But before Sophie could answer him, Coach Yates gave an extra-obnoxious blast on the whistle that brought even the Corn Pops out of their huddle.

"Singletary!" Coach Yates yelled. Nobody could holler like Coach Yates. "Are you looking for a detention your first day? Get yourself down from there."

Sophie looked in the direction Coach Yates was yelling. Her mouth dropped open.

"Somebody's making a holy show of herself," Darbie said.

A girl with bright red hair was shimmying up one of the volleyball poles. Even with Coach Yates still shouting, the girl reached the top and looked down triumphantly at the entire seventh-grade PE class.

"Who is *that*?" Julia said.

Beside her, Corn Pop Anne-Stuart gave the usual sniff. Sophie wondered where all the stuff in Anne-Stuart's nose could possibly come from.

"She'd better get down," Maggie said. "She's gonna get in so much trouble."

"Is she mental?" Darbie said.

Sophie was sure of it when Red-Haired Girl suddenly let go of the pole and leaped to the gym floor. Her flight landed in a roll that brought her right to Coach Yates' feet. Vincent clapped — until Coach Yates shot him the Coach *Hates* look.

She ordered them all to get into their teams for warm-up and pulled Red-Haired Girl to her feet. Coach Nanini joined them—the big man Sophie thought of as Coach Virile. He had muscles as big as hams and one large eyebrow that ridged his eyes. He was the boys' coach, but Sophie secretly called him hers.

Sophie tried to hear what he was saying to Red-Haired Girl in his high-pitched-for-a-man voice, but Coach Yates blasted the whistle yet again and sent them all scurrying. The Charms went to get a ball while the Corn Flakes gathered on their court.

"What was *that* about?" Fiona said.

"She'll get double detention for it," Maggie said.

Fiona rolled her eyes. "That's, like, something my little brother would do."

"So's that," Darbie said, nodding toward Coach Nanini and Red-Haired Girl. The girl was rolling the front of her T-shirt onto her arms so that her bare belly showed. Somebody on another team yelled, "Woo-hoo!" Probably one of the Fruit Loops, Sophie thought. They were the boys famous for such talents as burping the alphabet, booby-trapping toilets, and far worse.

"She acts like she's in about fourth grade," Willoughby said.

With an eyebrow raised, Sophie looked around the circle.

"Oops," Darbie said. "We're breaking the Code, aren't we?"

Maggie gave a solemn nod, and Sophie knew she was about to list the entire Corn Flake Code for them.

"Never put anybody down even though they do it to you," she said as if she were reading it. "Don't fight back or give in to bullies; just take back the power to be yourself. Talk to Jesus about everything, because he gives you the power to be who he made you to be. Corn Flakes are always loyal to each other."

"I always make a bags of that 'don't put anybody down' part," Darbie said.

Kitty nudged her. "Shh. Here come the boys."

The Corn Flakes spread into a circle so the Charms could join them for warm-up. Nathan, the third Lucky Charm, soft-served the ball to Fiona, his face going strawberry-red for no reason at all except that he was Nathan.

"So what was with the girl on the pole?" Jimmy said.

"I think we're about to find out." Willoughby jerked her curls toward Coach Yates, who marched in their direction with Red-Haired Girl right behind her.

"Do you think she heard us?" Kitty whispered to Sophie.

"Not with that whistle going off all the time," Sophie whispered back.

Coach Yates stopped, and Red-Haired Girl plowed into the back of her.

"Team One," Coach Yates said to them, "meet Brooke Singletary."

Brooke rolled her forearms up in her shirt front again. Nathan turned scarlet.

"Hey," Brooke said. "I'm on your team now."

Sophie was sure Brooke must have a hundred freckles per square inch on her face. They seemed to jump around when she talked, just like the rest of her. Sophie wondered if she might have to go to the bathroom.

Fiona waved. "I'm Fiona," she said.

The rest of the group said their names, except Nathan, who just bobbed his head and went radish colored. Before they even got to Sophie, Brooke said, "I'm serving first," and snatched the ball from Fiona. Then she tore toward the serving corner of their court, untied shoelaces flapping.

"Yeah," Fiona said, staring after her, "why don't you just do that little thing?"

This, Sophie decided, was going to be a real test of their ability to uphold the Code.

Before all the Flakes and Charms could get into position, Brooke smacked the ball and sent it sailing just over the net. Colton Messik, a Fruit Loop, turned in time to smack it back over. Maggie jumped toward the ball, hands in perfect position to set it up, but a blaze of red was suddenly there. Brooke's head collided dead-on with Maggie's, and Maggie staggered backward. Jimmy stepped in and caught her.

The court burst into a chaos of shouts.

"You should have let her set it up —"

"You're supposed to play your position —"

"Are you gone in the head, girl?"

"You can let go of me now!"

That last shout came from Maggie, who squirmed away from Jimmy and glowered at Brooke. "That's not the right way to play," she said.

"I don't know," Tod Ravelli called from the other side of the net. "I thought it was slammin'!"

Colton and Tod did an instant replay of Brooke ramming into Maggie, and Julia exchanged lip-curled smiles with Anne-Stuart and Cassie.

"You okay, Mags?" Willoughby said.

While she and Kitty examined Maggie's forehead, Sophie watched Brooke. She tossed the ball in the air and stumbled after it, this time falling into Nathan, who went past red and into the purple color family.

"I think this might be beyond the Corn Flake Code," Fiona muttered to Sophie.

Sophie turned to Darbie, who was shoving her hair behind her ears, over and over.

"I think she needs some Round Table help," Sophie said to her.

Darbie directed her bird-bright dark eyes down at Sophie. "That's easy for you to say, since you're not on it, and I am."

"I'm a consultant," Sophie said, lifting her chin. "And I think I should *consult* with Coach Nanini."

Darbie sighed. "You're always so good, Sophie. I'd rather toss her out by her drawers and be done with it."

But Darbie followed Sophie to Coach Nanini, who was one of the Round Table advisers. Round Table was a council of faculty members and students who tried to help kids that couldn't seem to follow the school rules. Coach and the other teachers thought most kids acted out because something was bothering them, and instead of just being punished, they should be helped. Sophie had been on Round Table for the first half of the year until a new council came on, but Coach and Mrs. Clayton, the other adviser, had asked Sophie to be a consultant.

"It's Little Bit and the Lass," Coach Nanini said when they reached him. "Those are some serious faces."

"That's because we have a serious problem," Darbie said.

Coach Nanini folded his big arms and said, "Okay, let's hear it."

Sophie filled him in, while Darbie punctuated with little grunts. When she was finished, Coach Nanini peered beneath his hooded brows in the direction of Team One's court. The ball was just sailing from Tod Ravelli straight to Brooke—who had her back to him as she gawked at Kitty on the sideline waiting to rotate in.

"Heads up, Brooke!" Fiona shouted.

But the ball hit Brooke in the back of the head and bounced away. "Hey!" she said. "What jerk threw that at me?"

Coach Yates blasted the whistle, and Coach Nanini nodded his shaved head. "She looks like Round Table material to me. I'll talk to her after class."

15

Sophie felt a wisp of guilt as she and Darbie joined the team again. *I feel like I just passed Brooke off so we wouldn't have to deal with her,* she thought.

But by the time Coach Yates sent the class to the locker room, all traces of regret had disappeared. Within thirty minutes, Brooke had fallen into the net, told Vincent he had big lips, and wrestled Fiona for the ball until Coach Yates nearly popped a blood vessel blowing her whistle.

"I know this isn't Corn Flake Code," Fiona said to Sophie as they headed for the locker room, "but that girl is harder to be around than the Corn Pops."

"Maybe she has issues," Sophie said.

"Yeah, well, if she ever tackles me on the volleyball court again, she'll definitely have an issue." Fiona sighed and rolled her eyes. "Okay. I'll pray for her. Besides . . ."

But Sophie didn't hear the rest. She pulled Fiona to a stop by the sleeve and pointed.

"My sister's here," Sophie said, her voice cracking. "This can't be good."

Lacie was standing in the doorway to Coach Yates' office, looking way too serious for a fourteen-year-old. Even the scattered freckles across her nose looked pinched in.

"Lacie?" Sophie called.

Her sister turned toward her with tears in her eyes. Lacie never cried. "We have to go to the hospital," she said.

"Is the baby born yet?" Sophie said.

"Yeah, and Soph—I think there's something wrong with her."

Two

Boppa, Fiona's grandfather, was waiting in front of the school to take the LaCroix girls to the hospital. Sophie was full of questions for Lacie as they hurried to his car.

"How do you know something's wrong with the baby?"

"I just—"

"Did you talk to Mama?"

"No, but—"

"Did Boppa tell you?"

Lacie shook her head, swishing her dark ponytail from side to side. "He just said Daddy needed to stay there with Mama. That alone tells you something."

"What does it tell me?" Sophie said.

"That something's not right."

"Not really," Sophie said. "Maybe the baby's just so adorable Mama couldn't wait till after school for us to see her."

Lacie gave her a big-sister look before she opened the car door. "Right. Daddy's going to take us out of school for that. Frogs might sprout wings and fly too."

Sophie slid into the second seat of Fiona's family's SUV. Boppa, who was usually ready with a grin and a wiggle of his caterpillar eyebrows, looked at her as if his soft face were about to crumple. Hard fingers of fear wrapped themselves around Sophie's heart and stayed there.

"Okay, Mr. Bunting," Lacie said as she buckled herself into the front passenger seat. "I wish you'd tell us what's going on."

Boppa shook his partly bald head. "Your dad just wants everybody together for your baby sister."

Lacie gave Sophie a what-did-I-tell-you look over the front seat.

Poquoson, Virginia, and then Hampton seemed to pass in slow motion as they rode through the February bleakness, but Sophie's mind was on fast-reverse.

Mama had had to stay in bed for the last several months because Baby Girl LaCroix wanted to be born too soon.

Nobody was supposed to upset her—and Sophie was sure she had at least a dozen times—not to mention the trouble her six-year-old brother, Zeke, had gotten into pretending to be Spider-Man. Had they caused the baby some kind of problem?

Mama had gotten paler and puffier, and early that morning when Daddy took her to the hospital she'd looked even worse to Sophie—like a bloated marshmallow.

Did all that mean the baby was born sick?

Or that Mama herself had something wrong?

Sophie groped in her mind for a daydream character to escape into. Ever since the Corn Flakes had started making movies early in sixth grade, Sophie's dream people had become as real to her as actual people. They almost always became the main characters in their films, even after the Lucky Charms joined them in Film Club. Dr. Peter, once her therapist and now her Bible study teacher, had told Mama and Daddy that Sophie should always use her imagination. He believed that doing productions would help her channel it instead of letting it get her in trouble for daydreaming.

If the Flakes and Charms were working on a film right now, she could dive into her role as a superhero or something and imagine her way through this baby thing somehow.

But when Boppa took Lacie and Sophie to Daddy inside the hospital lobby, it was all too real. Their tall, big-shouldered father was white-faced, and his mouth was pressed into a line that quivered at the corners. His short dark hair looked as if he'd been raking his fingers through it.

Daddy held out both arms and folded the girls into them. Sophie thought he smelled nervous, like sweat and coffee.

"What's going on, Dad?" Lacie said.

He didn't answer for a minute, and when he did, his voice was thin. Very un-Daddy-like.

"We have a new LaCroix," he said. "Hope Celeste. Six pounds, one ounce." His arms squeezed tighter. "She's beautiful, just like her big sisters."

"Is she okay?" Lacie said.

There was a pause so long that the fingers of fear had another chance to grip Sophie's heart.

"She *will* be okay." Daddy loosened his hold so they could look up at him as they walked down the hall. "They're doing some tests."

"Tests for what?" Lacie said.

Sophie couldn't grab hold of any of her darting thoughts. Only one came out of her mouth. "She isn't going to die, is she?"

"Hel-*lo*—no!" Lacie said.

Daddy stopped them just outside a door and smothered Sophie's shoulder with his hand. "That's a fair question, Soph," he said, "and we think the answer is no. But she has to be checked because—"

His voice broke, as if something had chopped the words off in his throat. Sophie clutched at his big hand.

"Because," he said, "Hope was born with something called Down syndrome."

Lacie gasped right out loud.

"What is Down syn-whatever?" Sophie said.

"It means she'll be re—um, mentally challenged, right?" Lacie said.

Sophie stared, first at her, and then at her father.

"I'm not sure of everything it means," Daddy said. "She'll learn slower than other kids, and she'll look a little different."

"Like the kids in the Special Olympics," Lacie said.

Sophie had no idea what that was, but she could tell from the way Daddy nodded with his eyes closed that the "Special" was like the special in "Special Ed." Like the kids whose classrooms were near the Corn Flakes' lockers—the kids the Pops and Loops referred to as "'tards" and imitated behind their backs.

Then what Lacie had started to say was true. Baby Hope was retarded.

"Do you want to see her?" Daddy said. "Mama's asleep, but she said to let you meet Hope as soon as you got here. She knew you'd be excited."

Excited wasn't exactly the word Sophie would have used. She pulled a strand of hair under her nose, a thing she always did when she was confused. Her heart beat double-time as she followed Daddy through the door into a small hallway lined on one side by a window.

The room on the other side of the glass was softly lit. It took Sophie a moment to realize there was a clear, small, bathtub-style container just beyond the window. In it was a tiny, pink, kicking baby, waving her fists.

"That's your little sister," Daddy whispered.

Sophie was afraid to even peek at her. What if she had a giant head or two noses or something?

"Oh—she's adorable," Lacie said. "She looks like you, Sophie."

"Yup. Spitting image of you when you were born," Daddy said.

Sophie shuddered. *How can she look like me?* Sophie knew what "special" kids looked like. She stood on tiptoe to peer into the baby's bed, and she could feel her eyes bulging.

"Did I have all those tubes in me?"

"You had more," Daddy said. "You were really sick."

"Did I have Down syndrome too?"

Daddy pulled Sophie almost roughly to his chest and held on. "No, Baby Girl," he said. His voice sounded broken again. "You didn't have it."

"I'm talking about her hair and her little cheeks," Lacie said. "Check it out, Soph."

Sophie tried to look past the tiny mask over baby Hope's nose and mouth and the tube that fed into a vein in her little head. She did have a fuzz of golden hair, almost like a miniature halo. Her skin was pale with a whisper of pink, just like Sophie's and Mama's. And she was tiny—the tiniest person Sophie had ever seen.

"She's going to be the shortest one in the class, just like me, isn't she?" Sophie said.

"If she ever goes to schoo—"

"Lacie," Daddy said.

Sophie glanced back to see Lacie biting her lip.

"Let's go see if Mama's awake," Daddy said.

Sophie took another long look at her baby sister, who had drifted off to sleep. She didn't have as many things going in and out of her as Kitty had had when Sophie visited her in the hospital. That had to be a good sign. And although Sophie hadn't seen all that many newborn babies, Hope looked perfectly normal to her. All the fingers and toes were there. She had two eyes. Her ears were sort of rolled up, but maybe that was because they weren't all the way open yet. When Darbie's dog had puppies, it took two weeks for their ears to pop into shape.

"Come on, Soph," Daddy said. He smiled a tired smile. "You'll be able to look at her for the rest of your life."

Mama was sitting up in bed when they got to her room, and her face was pinker and less puffy than Sophie had seen it in a long time. She almost looked like regular Mama again, except that Sophie could tell she'd been crying. That was *not* a good sign.

"Is she getting more beautiful by the minute?" Mama said as she hugged Lacie.

"Yes—even though she does look like Sophie." Lacie grinned back at Sophie and wrinkled her nose.

Sophie edged carefully up to the bed to give Mama a kiss. Mama pulled her right into her arms.

"I won't break, Dream Girl," Mama said. "I'm going to be back on my feet any minute now. Then we can get back to normal, huh?"

Lacie looked at Daddy, who cleared his throat.

"You told them," Mama said to him.

Daddy nodded.

"It's not ever going to be normal again, is it?" Lacie said.

Sophie thought her heart would squeeze to a stop.

"It's going to be a new normal," Daddy said. "Our little rookie will have special needs, and we'll learn how to meet them. We'll work together as a team. New game plan, that's all."

Daddy always talked about the family like they were headed for the Super Bowl. But the tears sparkling in his eyes weren't part of his usual game face.

"The first thing we're going to have to do," Mama said, "is make sure Zeke doesn't use Hope for a football."

"Or try to climb up the wall with her like Spider-Man," Lacie said.

"She might be the first Spider-*Baby*." Daddy laughed. It sounded like a laugh he had to make up, because he couldn't find a real one.

"It's going to be okay, my loves," Mama said. "God will show us everything we need to know."

She put out her hands for the girls to take hold. Mama's was icy cold in Sophie's. Daddy's was clammy. It made Sophie wonder if they really believed it would be okay at all.

Sophie tried that night to imagine Jesus before she went to sleep. That was what Dr. Peter had taught her to do. With Jesus' kind eyes in her mind, she could tell him and ask him anything she wanted. She didn't imagine his answers, though, because Dr. Peter said that would be speaking for him, instead of waiting for the truth to appear in the days to come.

Sophie couldn't have thought up answers for Jesus that night anyway. She couldn't even think up questions. It was so confusing, and all she could do was fall into a restless sleep. When she woke up the next morning, she was holding her hair under her nose again.

Zeke flew into Sophie's room and threw back the filmy curtains that hung around her bed.

"Daddy's taking us out for breakfast!" he announced. His volume was always on LOUD.

Sophie tried to pull one of her purple-and-pink pillows over her head, but Zeke yanked if off and sailed it across the room. He was dressed in full Spider-Man garb, including a red mask that covered everything except his eyes, and unfortunately, his mouth.

"Daddy's not gonna let you wear that into a restaurant," Sophie said.

"We're goin' to Pop's Drive-In!" he shouted. "You can wear anything you want. I'm even wearin' it to the hospital." He threw himself onto Sophie's bed and kneeled over her on all fours. "Hopey doesn't know about Spider-Man yet."

"But she's about to find out," Lacie said from the doorway. "Hurry up, Soph."

Lacie coaxed Zeke out with promises of cartoons. Sophie put another pillow over her head—because uninvited thoughts were barging in.

Would this be the last time they got to go to Pop's for breakfast? Would they be able to take Hope out in public if she was—different?

Sophie tried again to imagine Jesus with his kind eyes, and there he was. Only his eyes were sad, as if he didn't think everything was going to be okay, either.

That made it hard to climb out of bed.

When they got to the hospital, Daddy dropped Zeke off in Mama's room. He and Sophie and Lacie headed for the nursery to say good morning to Hope.

Sophie held a hunk of hair under her nose all the way down the hall. The closer they got to the nursery, the slower she walked. By the time she reached the window, Daddy and Lacie were already there, waving excitedly to someone on the other side of the glass.

"Look who's up!" Lacie said.

Sophie slid reluctantly between her and Daddy, to see a nurse in a mask holding Hope in her arms. The tubes that had been taped to the baby's face were now gone.

"She's breathing on her own," Daddy said. "Look at that—she's doing it."

"She's amazing," Lacie said.

Sophie couldn't take her eyes off the tiny person's face. Without half of it covered, Sophie could see a nose so small it almost didn't exist. Unlike Sophie's eyes, the baby's murky-blue eyes tilted up a little at the outer corners. From her baby-pink mouth, a matching tongue poked out. And stayed there.

"She's so precious," Lacie said.

"Her eyes will probably turn brown like yours did, Soph," Daddy said.

But Sophie could barely keep from crying out, *It's just like you said, Daddy. Our baby is different.*

The nurse let Daddy in so he could hold little Hope, and Lacie pressed her hands and nose against the glass. Sophie backed silently away and walked, stiff-legged and fast, until she found a cubicle that said FAMILY WAITING ROOM on the door.

She plopped down on one of the sofas and closed her eyes. But she couldn't erase the picture of her baby sister with a tongue that lay on her lips like a wilted rosebud. It reminded her of kids she'd seen at school who couldn't control their own faces and bodies.

Is she always going to look like that? Sophie thought.

How was she supposed to eat?

How was she going to talk?

Sophie squeezed her eyes shut tighter. Would she ever even learn to talk? What about all the dreams the Corn Flakes had had of teaching her to use Fiona-vocabulary—like "dire" and "fabulous" and the Corn Flakes' favorite, "heinous"?

Sophie watched those dreams swirl away down an imaginary drain, but she shook her head. It would be at least two years before even a normal little kid could say those words. Maybe there would be a cure for Down syndrome by then. Maybe Sophie would be the first one to read about it and tell Hope's doctor. Maybe she would even—

The doctor straightened up from the microscope and worked hard at not smiling—at not running around the laboratory, shouting, "I've found it! I've discovered the cure!" After all, she couldn't be completely sure yet. There were more tests to do. And if she revealed how close she was now, it would be in all the news reports, because everyone had complete faith in her work. She could already see the headlines: DR. DEVON DOWNING FINDS CURE FOR DOWN SYNDROME.

But fame was not the reason the good Christian doctor was so devoted to this work. If she could just see one Down syndrome child's eyes and ears and tongue become normal, if she could hear one say "heinous" and know that one was enjoying breakfast at Pop's Drive-In on a Saturday morning, it would all be worthwhile.

Dr. Devon Downing picked up her notebook of findings. She must make sure that she was as close as she thought she must be to—

"What are you doing down here reading a magazine?" Lacie said.

Sophie looked up with a jerk.

"The nurse said we could come in and hold Hope," Lacie said.

"Only one of us can hold her at a time." Sophie hugged the magazine to her chest. "You go first since you're the oldest."

Lacie put her hands on her hips, just like Daddy did when he was suspicious. "We can only hold her five minutes each, so don't take too long." She stepped back toward the door. "And since when do you read *Sports Illustrated* ?"

Sophie pulled the magazine out just enough to see the title.

"This isn't the best time in the world to be daydreaming," Lacie said. "Daddy said we all have to pull together as a family."

26

"I'm pulling," Sophie said.

Lacie disappeared, and Sophie tossed the magazine aside. It had been a long time since she'd gotten in trouble for lapsing into one of her imaginings and forgetting what she was supposed to be doing. It had hardly happened at all since Daddy had given her the video camera a year and a half ago. She knew if it became a problem again, he'd take it away.

Sophie sighed back into the sofa cushions. Would she even be able to make movies anymore? Was she going to be so busy pulling together with the family that she wouldn't have time to write scripts and act and direct?

Dr. Devon Downing straightened her white lab coat. There were always sacrifices to be made when a doctor was on such a quest as she was, but it was all right. "I will find a cure for Down syndrome," she said. "And that is all that matters."

"Wouldn't that be great?"

Once again Sophie jolted up, only this time Daddy stared down at her. He didn't put his hands on his hips, though. He sat beside her on the couch. Sophie had never seen dark smudges in the skin under his eyes before.

"I wish you or anybody else *could* find a cure, Baby Girl," he said.

"Somebody will," Sophie said. "They find cures for things all the time."

"Not for this." Daddy pinched the top of his nose with his fingers. "Whether a baby is going to have Down syndrome is decided way before she's born, when the chromosomes get handed out. They carry the genes that tell whether she's going to have brown eyes like you or blue ones like Lacie and Zeke. If she gets an extra chromosome, that decides she'll be—like Hope."

"Can't they just change the chromosomes or take one back out?" Sophie said.

27

Daddy shook his head like it hurt to move. "Once a baby is born with Down syndrome, that's it. She'll always have it. And no matter how hard you dream, Soph—there's nothing you can do about it."

Three

Sophie let everybody else in the family take turns holding baby Hope. Sunday morning she begged Daddy to let her go to church instead of the hospital, but he said they were having a special thanksgiving service for Hope in the hospital chapel, and she needed to be there. The only thing that made that bearable was that Dr. Peter was there too.

She spotted him right away, standing outside the chapel door. There was no mistaking his short gelled curls, his smile full of mischief, and the wire-rimmed glasses he always pushed up with a wrinkle of his nose. The eyes behind them twinkled when Sophie ran up to him, and the inner fingers that kept squeezing her heart let go a little. Any hard thing was easier with Dr. Peter on the scene.

"Sophie-Lophie-Loodle," he said in a hospital-low voice. "How's the big sister?"

Sophie's throat went tight. Dr. Peter nodded.

"What do you say we talk after this, huh?" he said.

That got her through the service. Lacie said it was pretty, with the candles and the tiny pink tea roses and the prayers Daddy and Mama and Dr. Peter said. All Sophie saw were the

29

tears behind Mama's and Daddy's smiles. She was ready to cry a few of her own when it was over.

Dr. Peter said, "Want to go downstairs and have a soda?"

The table and plastic chairs in the corner of the cafeteria weren't Dr. Peter's colorful office with its window seat and pillows with faces on them, but it didn't have to be. Once Sophie was seated across from him, a cherry Coke in front of her, she finally felt like she could tell someone everything. Still, she started slow.

"You know my little sister has Down syndrome," she said.

Dr. Peter pressed his lips together and nodded.

"I guess you know what that is."

"I do. Do you?"

"My dad told me. It can't be cured, you know."

"I know," Dr. Peter said.

The last piece of Sophie's dream was chipped away. She'd dared to hope that Dr. Peter, being a psychologist, would know something Daddy didn't. Right now, he looked as sad as everybody else.

"Are you scared, Loodle?" Dr. Peter said.

"Yes. Only don't tell my dad. We're supposed to be pulling together as a family."

"That doesn't mean you can't be afraid. Do you want to talk about why you're making a mustache out of your hair again? I haven't seen you do that in a while."

Sophie let her hair drop and took a sip of her cherry Coke. It didn't taste as good as it usually did.

"There's this new girl in my PE class."

Dr. Peter didn't ask her what in the world that had to do with her new sister, like most grown-ups would.

"She's out of control," Sophie said. "It's like she forgets there's anybody else around, so she runs all over, like, plowing into people and hitting them in the head with the ball. She can't pay attention, so she gets bonked with it too. And, seriously, she can't be still. I keep thinking she has to go to the bathroom."

Dr. Peter nodded.

"There's something way different about her—not, like, unique, but like something's wrong with her." Sophie discovered she had to swallow hard. "The other kids, you know, like the Corn Pops—"

"And the Fruit Loops?"

"Yeah—they all make fun of her. It's even hard for *us* not to say bad stuff about her. I bet she doesn't have any friends and—Dr. Peter?"

"What, Soph?"

The lump in Sophie's throat broke, and she felt her face wad up into tears. "I'm scared that when Hope goes to school, the kids are gonna be even meaner to her because she's—because she's—retarded!"

She pushed her Coke aside and folded her arms on the table so she could cry into them. Dr. Peter let her.

"Y'know, Loodle," he said, "I'd be worried about you if you *didn't* admit that you were afraid. Maybe mad too."

"Mad? At who?" Sophie said.

"Whoever's responsible for Hope being born with Down syndrome."

Sophie sat up straighter. "Who? What do you mean?"

"Remember when we first found out Kitty had leukemia?"

"Uh-huh."

"I told you when something happens that seems so unfair like that, instead of asking God *why*, it's better to ask, *what now?* I think that's what your dad means by pulling together as a family."

31

Sophie suddenly felt cold, as if she'd stepped right into her icy drink. "Are you saying you think *God* did this?" she said. "Oh—sorry. Is that bad to ask?"

"It's not a bad question, but that puts us back at *why?* and *who?*" Dr. Peter scooted his glasses up with a nose-wrinkle. "Do *you* think God made this happen?"

"How could he? Everything he does is for good, right?"

"We can trust there's a good purpose behind everything. And he's definitely in the *what now?* Do you think he'll help you know what to do with all this?"

Sophie couldn't answer right away. Other words—not very nice words—were in her head, shouting at her. She wasn't sure even Dr. Peter would want to hear them.

He leaned on the table, searching Sophie's face with his eyes. "Don't hold back, Loodle."

She looked away from him.

"You need to get this out—"

"I don't see why God didn't stop that one evil chromosome from getting into my sister," she blurted out. "Since he didn't stop it, maybe he's not involved at all. Not even in the *what now?* "

Sophie put the back of her hand up to her mouth. She would have given up her video camera just to have those words back.

But Dr. Peter didn't look disappointed. "You're having doubts."

"Yes, but I'm not supposed to doubt God. I mean, he's—God!"

"Which is why he can handle it. If you didn't have doubts, Loodle, you wouldn't ask questions. And if you never asked questions, you'd never get answers."

Sophie pulled her hair under her nose again.

"I know it's scary," Dr. Peter said. "But go ahead and pour out all that stuff to Jesus tonight when you imagine him. Tell him you don't know what to do next."

"He won't get mad?"

"Nah. Of course, don't expect the whole answer right away. You know how that works."

Sophie nodded glumly. Dr. Peter pushed her drink toward her.

"Now, about that wild thing in your PE class?"

Sophie blinked until she remembered Brooke.

"I doubt your little Hope is ever going to act like that. I don't know for sure without actually meeting the girl—"

"Brooke," Sophie said.

"Brooke. But it sounds to me like she *might* have ADHD—attention deficit hyperactivity disorder."

"I've heard of that," Sophie said. "Lacie says she thinks Zeke has it sometimes when he can't sit still."

"Zeke doesn't, but if Brooke does, she can't focus, can't stay on task. She gets distracted easily. She really can't help the impulse to do things without thinking about them first," Dr. Peter said. "The point is, your little sister won't act like that because her brain is very different." His eyes twinkled behind his glasses. "She'll probably be just as wonderful as you are."

Although Sophie finished her cherry Coke and the rest of the day without crying again, she felt dreary when she climbed into bed that night. She wasn't sure Dr. Peter was right about this telling-God-your-doubts thing, but he'd never steered her wrong before. She closed her eyes and tried to imagine Jesus.

She couldn't see his eyes, kind or sad or any other way. It was as if there was a fog separating her from the look she depended on.

Are you there? she asked in silence. *I mean, I know you are—it's just that I really need to know—how am I supposed to be a good big sister if I'm so confused?*

It wasn't at all what she'd intended to pray, and she still wasn't sure she should have prayed it at all. But Dr. Peter was right about one thing: there were no answers right away.

By the time third period came around on Monday, Fiona had already told Darbie about Hope. But Kitty, Willoughby, and Maggie arrived in the locker room with a banner that read CONGRATULATIONS BIG SISTER SOPHIE and enough candy pacifiers for all the Corn Flakes. Sophie took one look and burst into tears.

There was a lot of whispering as Darbie and Fiona filled them in. And then there was a lot of Corn Flake hugging and promising to help Sophie with *anything.*

"Thanks," Sophie said as they walked into the gym together. "But there isn't anything anybody can do."

Willoughby's eyes grew round. "I never heard you say that before, Sophie."

"Don't ever say it again, either," Darbie said. "You're scaring the bejeebers out of me."

A whistle blasted, which scared the bejeebers out of *Sophie.*

"Everybody up in the bleachers!" Coach Yates yelled.

"Will you be okay, Sophie?" Darbie whispered to her as they found seats.

Sophie didn't have a chance to answer.

"Do you smell something, Cassie?" Julia said.

Sophie stifled a groan, and Fiona nudged her in the side. The three Corn Pops sat in the row in front of them, all filing their fingernails.

34

"Yes, I do smell it." Cassie let her already-close-together eyes narrow. "Do you smell it, Stewie?"

"Definitely," Anne-Stuart said, with a juicy sniff. "I can't place it, though."

"Is it garbage?" Cassie said.

"Nuh-uh," Anne-Stuart said. "That's pooh if I ever smelled it."

"You're both wrong," Julia said. "That is the stink of somebody that lives in a ..." She curled her lip. "Mobile home."

"Eww," Cassie said.

Tossing her silky hair back, Anne-Stuart gave the longest sniff in sinus history. "Where's it coming from?"

Julia paused in her manicure and pointed a silver file with the jeweled head of a cat on one end. In spite of herself, Sophie followed it with her gaze toward the red head in front of Julia, next row down.

"That's heinous," Fiona whispered into Sophie's ear. "Brooke has to be able to hear her."

At that moment, Brooke stood up and snuffled into the air like a bloodhound. Darbie grabbed Sophie's knee. Fiona put her hand over Willoughby's mouth before she could poodle-shriek.

"I smell it too," Brooke said. She turned to Julia. "Want me to find out who it is for ya?"

Julia cocked her head of dark-auburn hair to one side. "Would you? I'd like to know so I can—uh—"

"Help them out a little," Anne-Stuart finished for her.

Cassie had already collapsed into a heap of giggles.

Brooke charged down the bleachers, stopping only to lean over and nuzzle at people with her nose. The girls the Corn Flakes called the Wheaties, because they were fun and athletic, reared away from her. Colton sniffed back and pretended to pass out on Tod. Nathan turned purple. Before Brooke could

35

start in on the student aide, Coach Yates blew her whistle and froze the whole gym.

"What in the *world* are you doing, Singletary?"

Brooke thrust a finger toward the Corn Pops. "She said she smelled somebody so I was just—"

"Just what?" Coach Yates said. "Giving everybody the sniff test?" She turned to Coach Nanini. "How about it, Coach? Why don't we all just choose up sides and smell armpits, huh?"

While the class erupted into hysteria, Sophie crossed her arms over her chest to keep the hard fingers of fear from squeezing her heart to death. No matter what Dr. Peter said, that could be Hope Celeste LaCroix down there someday, with even a teacher making fun of her. Coach Nanini bent his head low to talk to Brooke, but it didn't help Sophie. What if there was no Coach Virile for her sister? What if not one single person tried to help little Hope?

Coach Yates tooted the whistle again. "We'll review the volleyball rules for your written test tomorrow," she said. "I'm going to start on this end and drill you—"

That was the last thing Sophie heard Coach Yates say that period. She was too busy coming up with a plan. The minute Coach dismissed them, Sophie bolted for Brooke—who was perched on the bottom row of the bleachers, chewing on her fingernails.

"Hi," Sophie said as she sat beside her.

Brooke leaned over and tugged at Coach Nanini's sweatshirt. "Hey—Coach What's-Your-Name. Can I talk to her?"

Coach Nanini looked at Sophie and grinned. "Yes—she's the perfect person for you to talk to. Go change, and I'll see you back here after fourth period. We'll go together."

"Come on," Sophie said to Brooke. "I'll walk in with you."

Brooke looked Sophie over with green eyes that didn't stay any more still than the rest of her.

"We're on the same team," Brooke said.

"That's for sure," Cassie hissed as she sailed past.

Sophie caught sight of her Corn Flakes in the doorway, faces full of the question: *What are you* doing, *Sophie?*

I'm being decent to this poor kid, Sophie knew she would tell them later. *Because somebody has to.*

But when, for no apparent reason, Brooke pulled Sophie's glasses off and stuck them on her own face, Sophie wasn't quite sure why that somebody had to be her.

Four

Sophie had barely reached her locker when Brooke careened around the end of the row with her school clothes tucked under her arm.

"I'm changing here," she said as she threw her stuff on the bench.

"Sure," Sophie said.

"Won't they give you a locker?" Julia said from the other end of the row.

"She can change wherever she wants." Sophie patted the bench. "Here's a spot for you, Brooke."

Julia made a face and turned her back.

"Oh," Fiona said to Sophie, "I get it." Fiona gave a huff as if she were talking herself into something and looked at Brooke. "So — how come you just transferred into this class?"

"Where's my sock?" Brooke said, pawing through the pile she'd just dumped. "I can't find my sock."

"Maybe you dropped it on the way from your locker." Willoughby glanced at Sophie and added, "Want me to help you look?"

"I'll just borrow one." Brooke straightened up to face them. "Anybody got an extra sock?"

Sophie pulled out her toe socks, the ones with the turtles on the bottom. "You can borrow these. I don't need socks with my boots—"

"Sweet!" Brooke said and swept them out of Sophie's hand. She was feeding her toes into them before Sophie could finish her sentence.

Brooke still wasn't ready when Sophie left for fourth-period math class. Out in the hall, the Flakes were on her like Velcro.

"It's cool that you're being nice to her, Soph," Fiona said, "but you know I don't do nice as well as you do."

"She was digging through my bag," Willoughby said. "She said she lost her own brush."

"She looked at my hair all weird," Kitty said. She gave a nervous giggle. "I'm afraid she's gonna say something about it."

"I won't let her," Maggie said, words falling out like chunks of wood. "I won't be mean about it, but—"

"It's okay," Sophie said. "You guys don't have to be all friendly to her just because I am."

They all stopped at the end of the math hallway and looked at Sophie as if she'd grown an extra eye.

"Like we're really gonna let you do this by yourself," Fiona said.

"Hel-*lo*!" Willoughby said. "We're *all* Corn Flakes."

"Just don't expect me to be as patient as you are, Sophie." Darbie hooked her hair behind her ears. "When she gets to foostering and into everybody's things, I start to go mental. But if you just tell us what to do—"

"Hey—girl!" somebody yelled behind them. "Where's your fourth-period class?"

Brooke hurried toward them, her backpack half open with papers sticking out of it. One flew out and was immediately trampled by Brooke's own tennis shoe.

"I hope that wasn't important," Fiona said.

Brooke looked behind her and shrugged. "It's just my math homework. I didn't finish it anyway."

"Won't you get in trouble?" Maggie said.

Brooke shrugged again. Sophie noticed that her short neck disappeared when she did that. *She's sort of like a Raggedy Ann doll*, Sophie thought.

"You want me to zip your backpack up for you?" Willoughby said.

"Zipper's broken." Brooke looked at Sophie. "So—what's your name?"

"I'm Soph—"

"Dude!" Brooke stared toward the math room. "Is that your teacher?"

Sophie glanced at the very pointy Miss Imes, their math instructor, who was standing in the classroom doorway raising her arrowhead eyebrows at the students hurrying in.

"Yeah," Sophie said. "That's Miss—"

"What's *your* name?"

"Sophie!" the rest of the Corn Flakes said.

Brooke pulled her head back. "Dude," she said, "you don't gotta yell."

"That's it," Darbie muttered to Sophie as they hurried toward Miss Imes. "I'm going mental."

Although it wasn't good to lose focus in Miss Imes' class, Sophie couldn't concentrate that period. If she wasn't picturing Hope growing up and driving everybody "mental," she was imagining herself trying to have a conversation with Brooke, who obviously couldn't stay on one subject for more than half a second.

And then Sophie didn't *have* to imagine her, because Brooke was standing in the hall, outside the open door. She waved to Sophie with a grin that set all her freckles dancing.

40

"May I help you, young lady?" Miss Imes said.

"It's that weird chick," Colton said.

Miss Imes pointed a finger at him, even as she moved to the doorway. Sophie wanted to squirm right out of her skin.

Just don't let her tell Miss Imes she was waving to me, she prayed.

"I was just saying hi to somebody," Brooke said.

"Did your teacher give you a pass to come say hi to somebody?" Miss Imes's voice grew as pointy as her nose. "Or is there some other place you're supposed to be?"

Brooke bolted from the doorway. Miss Imes took off after her.

"Busted," Tod said and high-fived Colton.

Sophie looked at Fiona. Her bow of a mouth was drawn into a knot, and she shook her head. It was clearly an *I-hope-you-know-what-you're-doing* message.

The Corn Flakes discussed it at lunch, minus Darbie, who had a Round Table meeting.

"Okay," Fiona said. "Can we review the Corn Flake Code again?"

Maggie reached into her bag and, without even looking to see where it was, pulled out the Corn Flakes Treasure Book. Sophie knew she always kept the special purple notebook in exactly the same place. She guarded it like a CIA agent with a top secret document. After all, it held every one of the scripts for the eleven movies they'd made, plus the Corn Flake Code, and almost everything they'd ever said in a meeting that Maggie could write down in her slow, careful handwriting.

"You want me to read it out loud?" Maggie said.

"Not *loud* loud." Willoughby glanced over her shoulder.

Maggie read the code in a voice only slightly softer than her usual thuds. She looked up at the group.

Fiona poked her fork into a chicken tender. "It doesn't say we have to let the people we help get *us* in trouble."

"Who's in trouble?" Sophie said.

Fiona pointed the fork at her. "*You* would have been if Miss Imes had known who Brooke was out there waving to."

"That wasn't Sophie's fault." Kitty's giggle was nervous again.

"It doesn't matter with Miss Imes," Fiona said.

Maggie nodded solemnly. "Besides, if somebody gets in trouble, Sophie always gets in it with them."

"You in trouble, Soph?" Jimmy appeared and straddled the chair next to Sophie. Vincent and Nathan stood behind him.

"Not yet," Fiona said. "But if that Brooke child stays around, it's only a matter of time."

"We're being nice to her, though," Willoughby said pointedly.

"Don't look at *me*," Nathan said. "I'm not gonna be mean to her."

Sophie figured he wouldn't even look at her if he could help it. His face was already the color of a radish, and Brooke wasn't even there.

"We think she has issues," Maggie said.

"She's probably ADD," Vincent said. "Maybe ADHD. Or OCD."

"*What* are you talking about?" Willoughby said.

But Sophie nodded. Dr. Peter had said Brooke might have ADHD. Vincent probably read about it on the Internet.

Jimmy did a drum roll on the back of the chair. "So—we came to talk about a movie. Miss Imes asked me if we had anything going. Whatcha got, Soph?"

"Can we please *not* do a movie about ABCD or whatever it is?" Willoughby said.

"That could actually be cool," Vincent said, his voice cracking on the *cool*.

"No," Fiona said, "it would be heinous. I personally don't want to play the part of somebody that climbs up a volleyball pole in the middle of roll check."

Suddenly everybody looked at Sophie.

"*What?*" she said. Her own pip-squeaky voice went up almost as far as Vincent's.

"We know you, Soph," Fiona said. "So let's agree: no movie about being hyperactive, starring Brooke Singletary."

There was much holding of breath until Sophie nodded. "Okay," she said. "We can be nice to her and not put her down, but we don't have to include her in our next movie."

"That's a relief," Kitty said.

But Sophie didn't feel relieved. She felt ... well ... *itchy*.

"At least Darbie won't go mental now," Fiona said as they walked toward fifth-period science.

"I think she already has." Sophie pointed at Darbie, who was charging toward them. "Are you okay?" Sophie said when Darbie screeched to a halt in front of them.

"Thanks to *you*, Sophie," she said, "no, I am *not!*"

She stormed into the science room.

"What did I do now?" Sophie said.

"I'm afraid to ask," Fiona said.

But Sophie did ask, as soon as she could get to her desk and write a note to Darbie, which Fiona delivered to her while the smiling — and sometimes clueless — Mr. Stires took attendance. He was their science teacher and Film Club adviser. Everything about him was cheerful, including his gray toothbrush-shaped mustache.

Darbie, on the other hand, looked about as cheerful as the day after Christmas vacation. She flashed her dark eyes across Sophie's note, snatched up her pen, and scribbled on the paper with such force that Sophie was sure she'd engrave the letters into the desktop.

"We have a special lab tomorrow," Mr. Stires said. "You're going to dissect a lizard."

"Sick," Julia said.

While Mr. Stires assured Julia that the lizard would be freeze-dried, Darbie's note made its way to Sophie's desk.

Thank you VERY much, Sophie, for telling Coach Nanini that Brooke needed to go to Round Table. GUESS who he assigned her to. ME! I will absolutely go mad—I mean it. I said I would be nice—I didn't say I could fix her!

"I won't touch something dead, Mr. Stires," Julia said.

"I won't either," Anne-Stuart said. "It's against my civil rights."

"Try again," Vincent said. "That's not covered in the Constitution."

That conversation could go on for days, Sophie knew. She wrote back to Darbie.

Who guessed they'd assign her to you? But you'll be perfect.

Sophie pulled up a picture in her mind of B. J. Schneider, a former Corn Pop her "friends" had dumped on so badly, she'd transferred to a private school. Darbie had helped her—

Remember B.J.? Sophie added to the note.

Vincent was still on the Fourth Amendment. Fiona slipped the note to Darbie, who answered at the speed of light.

B.J. was completely different. In the first place, she didn't start chumming up to us like THIS girl. And B.J. didn't act retarded. I'm telling you, Sophie, Brooke is not the full schilling.

Sophie stared at the note until her eyes blurred with tears, but she could still see the word *retarded*. And she could see baby Hope in her mind. The fear fingers squeezed Sophie until she had to write—

She's mentally challenged—not retarded. And I'll help you—I AM the consultant—and we'll be so fabulous to her that she'll be cured.

"Hurry up, Soph," Fiona whispered. "Mr. Stires is about to give the assignment."

Sophie shoved the note across the desk. It came back just as Mr. Stires turned to write on the board.

I'm sorry I said retarded, Darbie had written, *but just so you know, after the way she acted at Round Table, I don't even want to be around her anymore.*

"Okay," Mr. Stires said, happily rubbing his hands together. "Be sure to answer all the questions so you'll be ready for your lizard tomorrow."

Dr. Devon Downing closed her eyes. She was weary to her bones, but she couldn't stop working. Maybe the lizard's brain would show her what she needed in order to find the cure for—for ADHD. Surely THAT wasn't in the chromosomes, like that other poor baby's problem. Dr. Devon opened her eyes and went straight to her text. Before she even touched the specimen, she would find that out—

"Good job, Sophie," Mr. Stires said. "Class, I want everybody working like Sophie's doing."

Sophie heard Fiona clear her throat. A cough had always been the signal for Sophie to pay attention and not drift off into Sophie World. Okay—she would read the assignment now, but when she got home, she was going to email Vincent.

Vincent sent her a list of what looked like a bajillion websites for ADHD, and most of the articles were hard to understand. Sophie had to keep stopping to look up words like *hyperactivity, impulsivity,* and *inattention.* She finally figured out that kids with ADHD were just like Dr. Peter described—they had trouble paying attention, got distracted, couldn't seem to follow directions, forgot information, and lost things. Kids with ADHD were just like Brooke.

What a devastating condition, Dr. Devon Downing thought. It's a wonder the poor child can even function in school.

Putting her luscious hair up into a bun and securing it with a pencil, she burrowed further into the articles, like the amazing medical researcher she was.

There was no cure for ADHD, the Internet told Sophie, but symptoms could be controlled if the child had lots of structure and routine, was rewarded for self-control, and had a very healthy diet. There was some disagreement, it seemed, over whether too much sugar made ADHD worse, but Sophie decided it couldn't hurt for Brooke to cut back.

She will be my test case, Dr. Devon wrote in her notebook. A plan was forming in her scientific brain. Perhaps there was no cure now, but there had to be a cure for everything. Even Down syndrome. But she shook that off. One brain issue at a time. And meanwhile, there was much she could do for Raggedy Ann-D-H-D. She would begin tomorrow.

Five

"Just give it a try for one day," Sophie said to Darbie on the way into the gym for PE the next morning.

"What am I supposed to do?" Darbie said. Her eyes were narrowed so far down, they looked like hyphens.

"I'll start by telling her the rules for taking a test in Coach Yates' class. If she follows them, we'll reward her."

"With what?" Fiona said on the other side of Sophie. "I, like, forgot my American Express card."

"We're supposed to give her money?" Kitty spiraled up into a whine.

"No," Sophie said. "Praise."

"Oh," Willoughby said. "Like, 'Good job,' 'All right, Brooke.' That kinda thing?"

"Yeah, just be her cheerleader," Sophie said.

Darbie sliced Sophie with a glance. "How about, 'Thank you for not crawling under me during the test and getting marker all over my leg. Excellent.'"

"She's not going to do that—is she?" Kitty said.

"She did it yesterday during Round Table." Darbie stopped inside the gym doorway, and the Corn Flakes huddled around her. "Coach Nanini and Mrs. Clayton had a bunch of colored markers so we could write out a plan for Brooke. She snapped them together into a tower until they broke apart and rolled under the table." Darbie rolled her eyes. "She dove down to get them and crawled right under my legs—"

"Nuh-uh," Kitty said.

"Yes. And somehow she got purple all over my calf." Darbie pulled up her pant leg to reveal a faded lavender blotch on her skin. "I was in the tub for an hour last night, and I still couldn't rub it off."

Willoughby out-poodled herself. Kitty giggled so hard, she collapsed into Maggie.

"I don't see what's so funny about it," Darbie said. She looked at Sophie, eyes like a pair of darts. "I'll give it one more day, and if she doesn't improve, I'm resigning from Round Table."

Coach Yates blew her whistle, so there was no time to protest. Sophie just prayed that her plan would work and climbed up the bleachers.

The average person does not understand how long these studies take, Dr. Devon reminded herself as she took her place in the great scientific arena. I must be patient and lead the way.

Sophie positioned herself behind Brooke and whispered the test rules to her while Coach Yates checked the roll.

"No talking—like, don't say a single word. Keep your eyes on your own paper. And don't move from your seat. Got it?"

"Yeah," Brooke said. "You got a pencil I could borrow?"

She is displaying all the symptoms, Dr. Devon Downing thought. I must record everything.

In the Treasure Book, Sophie thought. Since Maggie was already in test mode, she decided to fill her in later.

Meanwhile, there was a lot for her to remember about Brooke's behavior. The minute Coach Yates passed out the test papers, Brooke dropped the pencil Sophie had just given her under the bleachers and attempted to slip below to retrieve it. Coach Yates blew her whistle, making everybody in the silent gymnasium jump, and told Brooke to move down to the front row.

Two minutes later Brooke announced mondo-loudly that her pencil lead had broken.

Five minutes after that, Coach Yates caught her nudging Gill, one of the Wheaties.

"I just wanted to borrow an eraser," Brooke said.

Just as Coach Yates yelled out that time was up, *Brooke* yelled out that she'd erased a hole in her paper, and she needed a new one.

"Good job, Brooke," Darbie muttered to Sophie as they made their way down the bleachers. "You made it through the whole test without writing on anybody."

"Thanks," Brooke said—because she was suddenly right there with them, bouncing an eraser from one palm to the other. "I'm gonna eat lunch with you guys today."

Darbie's glare went right through Sophie's skin as Brooke bolted off to the locker room.

"I've been thinking about this film thing." Vincent came up behind Sophie and Darbie. He had Jimmy with him, and Fiona joined them.

Vincent's eyes had an idea gleam. "Why *don't* we do a film about ADHD?"

"I'd rather be shot," Darbie said.

"No, seriously. Mr. Stires wants us to do another project, and we could get extra credit in his class since we're studying the brain."

"I don't need extra credit," Fiona said.

Sophie sneaked a glance at Darbie. She could almost see steam coming out of her ears. But something about the idea did seem right—

"You have a new character." Jimmy's blue eyes sparkled at Sophie. "I've seen you thinking about her."

"Dr. Devon Downing," Sophie said.

Darbie groaned.

"She's looking for a cure for ADHD."

"And she needs a subject to study." Vincent wiggled his eyebrows.

"Oh," Fiona said. "Like Project Brooke."

"Only we can't tell her she's a project," Sophie said.

"She'll just be another character in the film," Jimmy said.

Darbie jammed her hair behind her ears so hard, Sophie was sure she would rip it out. "That's a flick I won't be participating in."

"Wait, Darb," Fiona said. "This could be your solution to helping Brooke for Round Table."

"I'm your consultant," Sophie said.

Darbie's eyes narrowed down to points. "Why do I feel like I don't have any choice?"

Sophie grinned. "I'll get my camera from Mr. Stires' room right after fourth period."

Everything at home was upside down over the next several days. Sophie was glad she had the film to concentrate on. Mama and Hope were still in the hospital, which meant Daddy was gone almost every evening to be with them, and Lacie was in charge. And *that* meant they ate macaroni and cheese (unless the other Corn Flakes' parents sent over casseroles) and rescued Zeke from every place Spider-Man could get to, including the rafters in the attic. Boppa finally rescued Sophie and Lacie and kept Zeke at his house until bedtime.

So Sophie was glad to become Dr. Devon Downing. She observed Brooke and trained the Corn Flakes to work with her during lunch and sometimes after school, when Brooke didn't have "something else to do."

"Like drive somebody else mental," Darbie muttered more than once.

On those days, with Brooke not there, they shot the scenes of Dr. Devon Downing and her able assistant, Test Tube Tess, played by Fiona. Darbie and Vincent filmed, Jimmy set up the shots, and Nathan stood around turning red.

Since there wasn't much makeup involved in the movie, which Willoughby usually handled, she concentrated on the praise-Brooke department. During PE, she'd say, "Go, Brooke—you almost hit it that time!" or "Yay—good job not stepping on Maggie!" Jimmy restaged that later for filming.

Fiona showed Brooke how to line up her clothes on the bench in the locker room so she wouldn't lose them. She rolled her eyes nearly up into her head when Brooke still ended up with somebody else's bra. That part Darbie didn't catch on film.

Maggie complained that there were no special costumes to make, but she quickly got the hang of reciting all the table rules for Brooke every day when they sat down to lunch in the cafeteria. No interrupting people. No talking with your mouth full. (Kitty's mother wanted to know why she was getting so much food on her clothes all of a sudden.) No borrowing lunch money. And no jumping up from the table every other minute. Footage of Maggie talking woodenly into the camera wasn't the best they'd ever taken, but Sophie said it had to be there.

Kitty became the best at rewarding Brooke with a small handful of Cheerios when she got something right. It seemed that Brooke would eat just about anything, including items from Darbie's lunch, when she wasn't looking.

"*You* weren't eating it," Brooke said when Darbie demanded to know where her brownie had disappeared to.

"I was *going* to," Darbie said, and then she gritted her teeth at Sophie. That was some of their best footage.

They got together without Brooke Thursday morning before school in Mr. Stires' room to check their progress on the film editor.

"This is some of our best stuff," Vincent said.

"It looks so real," Kitty said.

Maggie grunted. "It *is* real."

"Too bad it isn't working." Darbie's eyes were pointy. "As long as we're blathering at her," she said, "she does what she's supposed to. But the minute we look the other way, she starts foostering about again."

Now everybody looked at Sophie, and she felt prickly — the way she did when she had to take Lacie's turn with Zeke or the dishes. Why did she have to be responsible for everything on the planet?

"What does everybody else think?" Sophie said.

"What difference does it make?" Fiona said. "When it comes to doing the right thing, you always know."

"Do you think it would be right for us to just suddenly dump her?" Sophie said.

"Do you?" Willoughby said.

"No." Sophie knew her voice sounded prickly.

Vincent rubbed his hands together. "Then let's get back to work. Project Brooke could be our best production yet."

Sophie didn't say that she wished they'd stop calling Brooke a project. Or that she wished they wouldn't be so ready to give up all the time.

Or that she needed somebody *else* to come up with some answers for a change.

She just packed her camera into its bag and returned it to the shelf in Mr. Stires' storage room. Everything felt like a wool sweater itching her. She was afraid if she opened her mouth, she would scratch somebody.

But then, on Thursday, it looked like maybe Brooke was making progress. At the lunch table, almost before Vincent could get the camera rolling, Brooke sat down, pulled a sandwich out of a brown bag, and chewed an entire bite before she started talking.

"Good job!" Willoughby said.

Kitty dug into the huge box of Cheerios she'd gotten at Sam's Club. "You get a reward for remembering your lunch and not talking while you're chewing."

"All right!" Willoughby said.

"A reward?" Julia said.

Sophie looked up to see Julia and the Corn Pops standing at the end of the table with their trays. Sophie shook her head at Vincent, but he just pointed the camera at them.

"What is she, a puppy in training?" Cassie said.

"No," Brooke informed her. "I'm getting rewarded for not being rude."

Now would be a good time to hush up, Brooke, Sophie thought.

"Cheerios?" Anne-Stuart snuffled, taking away Sophie's appetite for cereal or anything else. "I'd hold out for M&Ms if I were you, Brooke."

Brooke snapped her head toward Kitty. "Yeah. How come I don't get candy?"

"Because sugar makes you even more—" Darbie started to say.

"Sugar isn't good for anybody," Sophie said.

"It's fine for me," Anne-Stuart said. She looked down at her twiglike body. "I never gain an ounce."

"Okay, I'm bored with this conversation," Julia said. With a toss of her thick hair, she whisked the Corn Pops away.

"I need something to drink," Brooke said.

She pushed her chair back so hard it banged into the kid behind her.

Sophie groaned. It was Tod Ravelli.

"Hey, step off, would ya?" Tod said. His spiked hair seemed to poke up taller as he stood his otherwise short self up. "That's like the eighth time you've touched me, chick." He put his face closer to hers. "I don't like to be touched."

Brooke looked at him for no longer than a millisecond before she gave him a poke in the chest with her finger.

"Hey, Brooke!" Sophie sang out as she shoved back her own chair. "Let's go get you a drink."

"He's a punk," Brooke said for all to hear.

Sophie put her hand in front of the camera and whispered, "Turn that off," before she led Brooke toward the drink counter. Brooke looked back over her shoulder.

"What's Tod doing?" Sophie said.

"Talking to that kid with the stick-out ears. They're both punks. I don't like punks." Brooke moved closer to Sophie as they walked—and didn't seem to notice that she pulled Sophie's shoe half off with the side of her foot. "But you," she said. "You I like."

"Oh," Sophie said. "Thanks."

But as Brooke filled a cup to overflowing with milk, Sophie wondered whether it was a good thing that Brooke liked her. After all, that wasn't the point of making this film with her. Was it?

"When do I get to see myself in the movie?" Brooke turned to Sophie and slopped milk over her hand and onto the floor. Sophie stepped back just in time to keep her tennis shoes from being drenched.

"Um, maybe after school—soon," Sophie said.

"Can't be Monday or Wednesday. I think I have to go to—" Brooke stopped and shook back her hair, splashing more of the contents of her cup. "Whatever. Anyway, I like movies. Can me and you go to one—like, a real one?"

Sophie was more than grateful when the bell rang. That way she didn't have to answer Brooke's question, or her own. What was she supposed to do if this hard-to-be-around girl wanted to be her new best friend?

All the questions made her want to scratch an itch she couldn't reach. That was not the way Dr. Devon Downing would handle it, she thought as she got ready for the lizard lab in fifth-period science.

A dedicated medical researcher such as myself does not have time to concern herself with these personal matters, Dr. Devon thought as she tucked her notebook neatly and professionally under her arm and headed for the laboratory. Today, for the first time, she was going to look into the brain of a lizard, and if things went as she hoped, she would find the final clue in her search for a cure. Then she would no longer have to worry about Raggedy Ann-D-H-D.

Dr. Downing's lab assistant, the devoted Test Tube Tess, uncovered the deceased lizard. It lay with its feet pinned down, ready to be opened up for medical science.

"We're supposed to cut from the neck down," Tess said.

But Dr. Downing placed the tip of her scalpel on the lizard's head and deftly spit it open. Although Test Tube Tess coughed loudly, there was no blood, nothing at all disgusting. Freeze-drying had taken all the grossness out of the procedure. Even if it had been a nasty job, Dr. Downing would have pressed on as she did now, peering at the reptile's tiny brain. The clue was in there; she could sense it. But it was far too difficult to see. She would have to extract—

Dr. Devon Downing skillfully pinched the brain with her tweezers and tugged. It was stubborn, so she pulled again, this time with more force. The tiny organ broke free, and Dr. Downing's arm flew back. There was a shocked silence, and then a cry —

"What *is* that?" Julia screamed.

"Where?" Anne-Stuart said.

"In my hair! It came flying at me! What is it?"

Vincent examined the top of Julia's tresses. "Looks like lizard brains to me."

Julia balled her hands into fists and screamed until Sophie was sure the noise would shear everyone's scalps off. "Get it out, Anne-Stuart!"

"I'm not touching it!"

"Get it out!"

"I'll get it out," Vincent said.

"Don't touch me!" Julia said.

Fiona looked slyly at Sophie from behind her hanging hunk of hair. "I wish we'd gotten that on film," she whispered.

That night, as soon as Sophie closed her eyes to imagine Jesus, Brooke was there instead.

That was the way it had been for a lot of nights now. Sophie tried to see her image of Jesus' kind eyes so she could talk to him and tell him how hard things were. But it was always something else she saw — like the little tongue her baby sister couldn't control, or the shenanigans (as Darbie called them) that Brooke couldn't control. Not being able to "see" Jesus the way she had before made it harder and harder to believe he was listening when she told him how everything was changing, and how scary it was.

She tried not to think her itchiest thought: that maybe he wasn't even there right now.

Six

It's one of God's miracles," Mama said that next Saturday morning. "She's just a little more than two weeks old. Even with all the problems they thought she had when she was born, she's home with us, healthy."

Sophie looked at the rest of the family, gathered in the family room around Lacie, who was holding Hope. She hadn't let go of the baby since Mama walked in the door with her from the hospital. Zeke was dangling a Spider-Man figure in the baby's face like he expected her to grab it and say, "Cool!"

Did no one else see that Mama didn't get it? Sophie thought. Hope wasn't healthy. She had something *huge* wrong with her.

"Okay, so here's the game plan," Daddy said. He clapped his hands together as if they were all about to take the field. "Everybody's going to want to hold the baby all the time, and that's good because we all love her." He looked straight at Lacie. "But she has to rest in her crib sometimes, where she can stretch out."

Lacie wrinkled her nose at Daddy and gazed down at Hope as if she were *her* baby. *Maybe nobody'll notice that I'm not holding her*, Sophie thought.

"When can she play?" Zeke frowned at Hope. "You sure sleep a lot."

"I tell you what," Mama said. "It's time for a bottle, so why don't we let Sophie feed her, since she hasn't had a chance yet."

"Sorry, Lace," Daddy said. "You're going to have to hand her over to your sister."

Sophie felt her face freeze. *I'm not ready for this!* she wanted to tell him and Lacie and anyone who would listen.

But everybody was scrambling around, putting pillows in place for Sophie to prop her arm on and warming a bottle in the microwave. Mama rewrapped Hope in her blanket so she looked like a little burrito with a tiny golden head. Before Sophie could escape into Dr. Devon Downing or anyplace else, she was on the couch, arms positioned like Lacie showed her.

"Be careful of her head," Lacie said. "You have to support it because she's not strong enough to hold it up by herself yet."

"Lacie," Daddy said from behind the couch, "why don't you go see what your brother is doing? We've got it handled."

The first thing Sophie noticed when Lacie placed Hope in her arms was how warm the baby was. The second thing was that she immediately wiggled and drew her face into a knot.

"What's going on?" Sophie could barely hear herself, her voice was squeaking up so high.

"She's hungry," Mama said. "Personally, I think she can smell formula from a mile away. Here you go."

She handed Sophie a warm plastic bottle. Hope made a sound like a baby bird and opened her tiny mouth so wide it seemed to fill her whole face. Her tongue pointed at Sophie.

"Just put the nipple in," Mama said, voice soft. "She'll grab onto it."

Sophie aimed the nipple for Hope's mouth, but it wasn't as easy to get in as Mama said. Her tongue was in the way.

"Just wiggle it around a little," Mama said. "Down babies sometimes have trouble with those tongues—keep trying."

Sophie tried pointing the nipple at an angle, but Hope's tongue was still right there. She scrunched up her face and gave an angry squawk.

"Hang in there, Little Rookie," Daddy said. "Sophie's working on it."

Sophie made another attempt and got the nipple in, but Hope spit it back out.

"Maybe she wants you to feed her," Sophie said to Mama, holding out the bottle.

"You'll be fine," Mama said. "I had trouble the first time too. Just press down a little on her tongue—there you go!"

The bottle slid in, and Hope sucked at it.

"Look at her eat," Daddy said as he leaned over the back of the couch. "That's my rookie."

"Now you can both just relax and enjoy," Mama said.

A shout erupted from the kitchen, followed by Lacie shouting back, "Spider-Man does *not* eat bugs, so get that nasty thing out of your cereal!"

"I'm on it," Daddy said and headed for the kitchen.

"You're doing great, Soph." Mama put her arm across the back of the couch. "She's very content right now."

Sophie looked down at her little sister, who was staring straight ahead as she drank. Her eyes were still a murky color, and Sophie couldn't tell if she was really seeing anything. Could a baby with Down syndrome see like everybody else? What if the whole world looked different to her? Was that one reason she'd be—mentally challenged?

Without meaning to, Sophie's arms tightened. Baby Hope stopped sucking on her bottle and thrust out her tongue. With it came a stream of white stuff that splattered all over the blanket.

"She's throwing up!" Sophie said.

"That's just a little dribble," Mama said. "Just tilt her up a little bit—"

"No, you take her, okay? I'm doing it wrong."

"Sophie, honey—"

"Here!" Sophie pushed the upchucked-on bundle of a baby into her mother's arms.

"I'll go get a washcloth," Sophie said.

"You don't need to. I have a wipe right here—"

Sophie ignored her mom and bolted for her room.

Sophie decided it was the longest weekend she'd ever lived. She spent a lot of it in her room, pretending to do homework, but mostly imagining Dr. Devon Downing so she wouldn't have to think about her baby sister.

But even that didn't work entirely. There was a constant hubbub of Hope wailing and Mama showing Lacie how to change diapers and Daddy telling Zeke what toys he could and could not put in the crib with the baby.

"She needs stuff to play with," Zeke said at least a hundred times.

And every time, Sophie thought, *Will she ever really hold things and play?*

She and the Corn Flakes had dreamed of teaching her little sister the joys of imagination, of becoming whatever she wanted to be. Thinking it might never happen made the fingers of fear curl around Sophie's heart tighter than ever.

By Monday, Sophie could think of only one thing to do to keep the fear away, and that was to concentrate on something else: Project Brooke. First, Sophie had to figure out what to do about Brooke wanting to be attached at the hip. Sophie just wasn't ready for that. Besides, even though they were almost finished filming, Brooke still hadn't shown as much improvement as Sophie needed to see. They needed more time.

"Maybe we should get some footage of her in some of her classes," Sophie said to the Corn Flakes on the way to third period.

"I never even see her in the halls," Willoughby said.

They all agreed that was strange, since Willoughby could hardly walk two steps without somebody saying hi to her.

Dr. Devon Downing made a mental note to get into the database and find Raggedy Ann-D-H-D's schedule. She felt a bit uneasy, but she chased that away. A medical researcher had to do whatever it took to gather information. It was for the good of all children with mental defects.

"There she is, right over there," Maggie said, pointing to the locker room door where Brooke was swinging, hands gripping the doorknobs and knees clamped.

"We should get some film of that." Kitty giggled.

"We have enough pictures of her shenanigans," Darbie said. "We need some of her improving."

Sophie sighed and headed for the door. When Brooke looked up, every freckle on her face seemed to darken.

"Hi," Sophie said.

Brooke watched as if she expected Sophie to pick her pocket. "What?" she said finally. "You're looking at me weird."

Actually, Sophie thought, *you're the one who's looking at me weird.* The suspicion in Brooke's eyes made her uneasy. "Um," she said, "want to do some more work on our movie with us?"

"You already took like twenty hours of me eating lunch."

Sophie blinked. *Okay,* she thought, *what happened to Brooke sticking on me like a shadow?*

"What if we filmed you in one of your classes?" Sophie said. "Do you have a teacher that's cool? We could ask her if we could do some shots of you at your desk—"

"No!" Brooke let go of the door handles and staggered backward. "I hate my teachers!"

She stumbled into the locker room and let the door close in Sophie's face.

"That went well," Fiona said in a dry voice.

But Sophie nodded. "That's like what I read about ADHD. Kids who have it don't do well in school because they can't pay attention, so they hate it."

"Don't even think about us helping her with her homework, Sophie," Darbie said. "Or I know I'll eat the head off her for sure."

"Okay, forget that," Sophie said. "We'll think of something else."

"*You* will," Willoughby said.

But Sophie didn't. When they got to the gym, Brooke was sitting on the floor, surrounded by Corn Pops.

"*That* can't be good," Fiona muttered to Sophie.

"I bet they're making fun of her," Kitty said.

Maggie shook her head. "Doesn't look like it to me."

It didn't to Sophie, either. Brooke was chattering nonstop, as usual, while Julia appeared to be giving her a manicure and Anne-Stuart coaxed her strings of red hair into a French braid.

"I *know* the Corn Pops." Willoughby twisted one of her own curls around her finger. "They wouldn't be nice to Brooke if they didn't want something from her."

Fiona raised an eyebrow. "No offense, but what does Brooke have that they would possibly want?"

"I don't know," Sophie said, "but we should find out. She *is* our project."

Darbie groaned. "I was afraid you'd say that."

Coach Yates blasted away on the whistle, and the Corn Flakes hurried to their line. Brooke passed them on the way to her place, but she didn't look at Sophie or any of them.

"She has something stuffed under her shirt," Maggie said. She demonstrated, pulling her own shirt out at the waist.

Sophie glanced back at Brooke, and her gaze snagged on Julia. Her eyes were gleaming with that hard kind of mirth Sophie knew was trouble. Whenever a Corn Pop thought something was funny, it was usually at somebody else's expense.

As soon as roll was taken, the Corn Flakes swarmed to their volleyball court and took the Lucky Charms aside.

"We're trying to find out what Brooke's got under her shirt," Sophie whispered.

Nathan's face went straight to red.

"No, silly." Willoughby poked him. "She's got something stuffed into the waistband of her track pants."

"Something she's not supposed to have," Maggie said.

"At least that's what we think," Darbie put in.

Fiona rolled her eyes. "If she got it from the Corn Pops, it's definitely contraband."

"What's that?" Kitty said, eyes wide.

"Something she's not supposed to have," Fiona said.

"Here she comes," Jimmy whispered. "What do you want us to do?"

"I'm not pulling something out of her shirt," Nathan said.

"Get her to jump up and down a lot," Sophie said. "Until it falls out."

"Done," Jimmy said.

It wasn't hard. Although Brooke was unnaturally quiet at first and volunteered to stand out and rotate in, they weren't two volleys into a game with the Wheaties' team before she was bouncing like the ball itself and yelling, "That was out! That was *so* out!"

"How about getting it for us?" Vincent said. "It went over there."

Brooke bounded after the ball, and Sophie watched the lumpy-looking bulge under her T-shirt shift to the side.

"I hope it doesn't go down into her pants instead of out." Willoughby gave the expected shriek.

"Hey!" Brooke yelled. "Somebody, catch!"

She heaved the ball so hard she fell after it, right on her tummy.

"My candy!" she cried. "Aw, man!"

Brooke rolled over and yanked a plastic bag from under her shirt. Five different kinds of mini candy bars scattered over the gym floor.

"Dude!" Colton Messik shouted from the next court over. "It's rainin' chocolate!"

Fifty pairs of tennis shoes squealed as Coach Yates blew her whistle.

"Singletary! What are you doing with food in class?"

Sophie only had to look at Julia, Cassie, and Anne-Stuart to know. All three of their glossy upper lips were curled like Fruit Roll-Ups.

"I wonder how much of that she already ate," Maggie said.

If the theory that sugar might make ADHD behavior worse was true, Sophie figured Brooke had downed about a pound. She was crawling around on the floor like a crab, snatching up miniature Snickers and Three Musketeers and shoving them back into the bag.

"I'll relieve you of those, Red," Coach Nanini said as he stood over her.

Darbie looked at Sophie. "I'm sorry, but I wish he would relieve *me* of *her*."

Dr. Devon Downing sighed. It was difficult to make progress when other factors were constantly entering in. But she went on, because the work of a gifted medical researcher could not be abandoned. She had to find a cure, before Raggedy Ann-D-H-D was lost to the—

"Corn Pop Alert," Fiona said.

Sophie looked up in time to see Brooke dallying at the edge of the court where the Pops and Loops were playing. Anne-Stuart whispered something in her ear, which kept Brooke from seeing the ball flying at her until it smacked her in the head.

"Hey!" Brooke yelled at Tod, who was innocently whistling into the air. "I'll kick your—"

"Brooke!" the Corn Flakes shouted in unison.

"It's your serve," Jimmy said.

Brooke gave Tod one last killing look before she bounded back to them.

"Cheated death again," Vincent muttered.

Brooke didn't show up at the Corn Flakes' table at the beginning of lunch, and Darbie gave a happy sigh. "I like having a moment of peace," she said as Sophie handed her the camera bag.

"The moment's over," Willoughby said. "Here she comes. You have those Cheerios ready, Kitty?"

But Brooke stopped at the end of the table and didn't put her tray down.

"I'm sitting with Julia and them," she said.

Everybody looked at Sophie.

"How come?" Sophie said.

"Because Julia's gonna finish doing my nails."

"You hardly have any nails," Maggie said.

"Ma-ags," Willoughby said out the corner of her mouth.

"She's gonna give me fake ones," Brooke said. "She has this really cool file thing—her mom bought it for her at the nail shop—"

"The one with the cat on it?" Kitty said. "That *is* cool."

Nice work, Kitty, Sophie thought.

Brooke nodded, sending her pizza slice dangerously close to the edge of the tray. "She said it cost fifty bucks."

"That's a bit of a horse's hoof, I think," Darbie said.

"Huh?" Brooke said.

"That means Julia's exaggerating," Fiona said. "No nail file costs—"

Fiona was cut off when Brooke's body suddenly lurched forward and her plate crashed to the table. The pizza slice landed pepperoni-down in Sophie's lap, and the contents of a glass of chocolate milk splashed up in Brooke's face. Brooke whirled around to find Tod Ravelli standing behind her, smirking.

"Sorry." His mouth was as unrepentant as anything Sophie had ever seen. "My bad. But you shouldn't be blockin' the aisle like that."

"You did it on purpose!" Brooke said.

Before Sophie could even agree, Brooke grabbed the now-empty tray and brought it down on top of Tod's head.

The cafeteria came to life with shouts of "Fight! Fight!"

Maggie and Darbie pulled Brooke by both arms, and Willoughby jumped on her back. Jimmy stood behind them, hands out like a baseball catcher. Vincent fumbled with the camera.

"Let me at 'im!" Brooke screamed.

"Don't do it!" Sophie tried to shout. But her pip-squeak of a voice was lost in Kitty's panicked cries, Fiona's attempt to talk

Brooke down, and the roar of the entire lunch room urging Brooke and Tod to go at it.

Only Coach Nanini could break up something like that, and he did. Then Mr. Bentley, the principal, hauled the kicking, screaming Brooke out. Mr. DiLoretto, the art teacher, dragged Tod in the direction of the nurse's office. Coach Nanini stood there, shaking his big head.

"Tod ran into her on purpose, Coach," Willoughby said. "We saw him."

"I didn't get it on film, though," Vincent said. "I was too late."

"That's okay." Sophie didn't like the weary sag of Coach Virile's eyebrows. "Red chose to take the matter into her own hands."

"Literally," Fiona said.

Coach gave a grim nod. "There are consequences for that."

"She's gonna get suspended," Maggie said when he was gone.

Darbie looked straight at Sophie. "I told you I didn't think our little project was working."

"What do we do now, Sophie?" Kitty said. She pointed to the cereal box on the table. "I have all these Cheerios."

Sophie felt irritated prickles go up her neck. "I don't know," she said as the bell rang.

"Maybe you'll figure something out by after school." Willoughby nodded until her curls bounced.

Sophie thought she might go "mental" instead from the nonstop itching inside her.

They had barely gathered at their lockers at the end of sixth period when Kitty said, "She's coming!" and ducked behind Maggie.

Brooke marched down the row of lockers, French braid half undone, waving a yellow slip of paper.

"I told you," Maggie said. "She got —"

"I'm suspended for three days!"

Brooke stomped up to Sophie and brought her foot down hard on Sophie's toe. Sophie choked back a yelp.

"Three days!" Brooke said. "And it's *your* fault!" She stormed off, still waving the suspension slip.

"That was just—violent!" Willoughby said.

Sophie sank to the floor and hugged her foot. "It's just because she's frustrated. I read that—"

"I don't care what she is." Fiona squatted beside Sophie. "I personally don't want to be around when she decides to break a tray over one of *our* heads."

"We have enough film to make our movie for class, don't we?" Darbie said.

Maggie consulted the Treasure Book and nodded. Willoughby and Kitty looked down at Sophie.

"Is it settled then?" Fiona put her hand on Sophie's arm. "Is Project Brooke over?"

No! Sophie wanted to shout at them. *I can't give up!*

But she didn't say anything at all.

Seven

The next day, Sophie was sure the rest of the Corn Flakes had taken her silence as a yes. And a yes, she quickly figured out, made everybody happier.

Kitty didn't nervous-giggle as much. Willoughby gave fewer poodle-yips. Darbie declared that she hadn't wanted to call anybody an eejit for a whole day.

So why, Sophie asked herself, didn't she feel all happy and free the way everybody else did now that Project Brooke was over?

One answer she knew right away. Without Brooke there, taking all of Sophie's attention, she couldn't keep her mind off baby Hope. What if nobody could help Hope when she got to be Brooke's age? What if people gave up on her and were glad when she wasn't around? The questions itched like poison ivy that was spreading.

Sophie only knew that if she gave up on Brooke, it would be like giving up on her own little sister. No matter what the other Corn Flakes decided, she had to be ready the minute Brooke came back.

Which was why, after school on Tuesday, Sophie went to the library and logged on to a computer back in the corner. The schedule of every student at GMMS was on a list anybody could pull up. She didn't even need Dr. Devon Downing for that.

Sophie scrolled through the R's and the S's until she came to *Singletary, Brooke.* She poised her gel pen over her notebook, ready to write down room numbers, but she couldn't take her eyes from the screen.

Period 1 — Special Education/Language Arts   Room 202
Period 2 — Special Education/Study Skills   Room 202
Period 3 — Physical Education   Gym

The rest of the classes were Special Ed too. There was even tutoring scheduled after school on Mondays and Wednesdays.

Sophie thought she had to be dreaming. She leaned closer to peer through her glasses, but the words were really there.

I don't remember the Internet saying kids with ADHD were Special Ed, she thought. In fact, she knew they weren't. One article had even said ADHD kids were just as bright as other kids, only they couldn't concentrate enough to get their work done. So what was going on?

Dr. Devon Downing pushed herself back from her microscope and used extreme willpower not to hurl it across the room. Once again, she was confronted with a medical mystery that perhaps she couldn't solve. Something else was wrong with Ann-D-H-D's brain, perhaps something that, like Down syndrome, couldn't be cured. No wonder the subject broke trays over people's heads and stomped on their feet —

"She's not a subject," Sophie said out loud. "She's a person — and I can't help her either."

She left the library before she started throwing books off the shelves.

The urge to throw things didn't go away. That night Sophie couldn't see Jesus' eyes again. She wanted to ask him her questions and belt out her doubts, but it all stuck in her throat.

Maybe he just didn't want to listen to her.

During the break between first and second periods the next morning, when Fiona, Darbie, and Sophie hung outside the classroom talking in frosty breaths, Fiona said, "Don't forget, we have Bible study this afternoon."

"My aunt's bringing snacks," Darbie said.

Sophie didn't say anything. Fiona nudged her.

"You're coming, right, Soph? Boppa's picking us up."

"I guess." Sophie shrugged.

Fiona and Darbie looked at her blankly.

"You guess?" Fiona said. "What's up with that?"

"I don't know," Sophie said. "Maybe I'm just tired of Bible study."

Darbie thrust her head forward. "Now *that's* a bit of the horse's hoof."

"Nobody loves Dr. Peter's class more than you do," Fiona said. "What's going on?"

"The bell's gonna ring." Sophie retreated into the classroom because she didn't want to tell her best friends that she was afraid to go to Bible study. They might all find out she was so mad at God, she wanted to grab an angel's harp and break it over her knee. Or whatever a person did when God didn't send any messages through Jesus that everything would be okay.

I must not allow these personal feelings to interfere with my research, Dr. Devon Downing scolded herself. What should I work on next?

"What do you mean?" Anne-Stuart said. "The assignment is right there on the board."

71

Sophie blinked and propped her social studies book in front of her, trying to focus on the page. All she saw was Dr. Devon Downing disappearing.

By the time they arrived at the church that afternoon, Sophie felt like a plastic bag full of air. One small punch would be all it took . . .

And Dr. Peter landed it the minute they were all situated in their different-colored beanbag chairs, Bibles in matching covers in their laps.

"So what's God been doing in your lives this week?" he said.

"Nothing," Sophie said. "I think he lost my address."

Everyone seemed to stop breathing at the same time. Sophie couldn't move, not even to say, *I'm sorry! I didn't mean that!* Well, she hadn't meant to *say* it, anyway.

Finally, Kitty giggled nervously, and Willoughby's poodle-yip came out as a whimper. Harley, one of the Wheaties, gave a soft snort. Everyone was looking at Dr. Peter, and even Sophie could see why. Nobody in the class had ever said anything like that about God before.

Dr. Peter sat forward in his beanbag chair and let his arms fall across his knees. "Is this something we need to talk about privately, Loodle?"

"Can I say something?" Fiona said.

Dr. Peter nodded at her. Sophie wished miserably that he hadn't.

"If Sophie's thinking that, then we all need to hear what you say."

"She's our friend," Kitty said in a tiny voice.

"Not only that," Darbie said, pushing her hair behind her ears. "If Sophie can go there, then the rest of us are bound to go there too, sometime or other. She knows God better than any of us."

"I thought I did," Sophie said. "Now I'm not so sure."

"Okay," Dr. Peter said. "If it's all right with you, Sophie, we'll all take a look at this doubt issue."

"Whatever," Sophie said. It was useless to keep pretending anyway, she thought. She'd already blurted out the worst thing she could possibly say.

"All right then." Dr. Peter rubbed his hands together the way he always did when they were ready to dig into the scriptures. "Let's open those Bibles to John 20, verse 26."

The air itself felt uneasy as the group thumbed its way to the New Testament. Usually Sophie loved this part and couldn't wait to hear who Dr. Peter wanted them to pretend to be in the story he read. But if it involved Jesus, she was afraid to even step into the scene.

"Imagine that you're the disciple Thomas." Dr. Peter pushed his glasses up with a nose-wrinkle. "Now, you remember that when Jesus rose from the dead, he appeared to the disciples in a locked house."

"John 20:19," Maggie said.

"Wow, Mags," Willoughby said.

"Thomas wasn't with them," Dr. Peter went on. "And when the other disciples told him they'd seen Jesus, he wasn't having any of it. He said unless he saw the nail holes in Jesus' hands and put his finger in them, he wouldn't believe it."

"Gross," Gill the Wheatie said.

"Now it's eight days later, and the disciples are all hanging out again. Thomas is there too, so pretend you're him."

Sophie automatically closed her eyes. Okay. She could be Thomas. All bristly and annoyed because he didn't see any evidence of Jesus anywhere. Sophie felt the fingers of fear. It wasn't really that hard to imagine right now, and that in itself was scary.

"'Though the doors were locked,'" Dr. Peter read, "'Jesus came and stood among them, and said, "Peace be with you!"'"

Sophie/Thomas looked up sharply. How did this intruder get in? The door was locked. Fear clutched his heart.

"'Then he said to Thomas—'"

Sophie/Thomas gasped. He's speaking to me! he thought. He clutched at the front of his robe. This couldn't be—Jesus was dead. He'd left them—abandoned them.

"'Put your finger here; see my hands.'"

Sophie/Thomas shuddered from head to foot. But he couldn't deny this man with the kind eyes who looked so much like his Jesus. Slowly he pressed his finger into the palm of the man's hand. It sank into a hollow, jagged hole. Thomas jerked back.

"'Reach out your hand and put it into my side.'"

Sophie/Thomas didn't want to, but something invisible seemed to push his fingers forward, until he could feel the gash where the Roman soldier had pierced Jesus with his sword—

"It's you!" Sophie/Thomas cried. "My Lord and my God!"

Sophie's eyes flew open. She'd almost forgotten Dr. Peter was reading. He looked at her over the top of his Bible. "'Then Jesus told him, "Because you have seen me, you have believed; blessed are those who have not seen and yet have believed."'"

Maggie raised her hand. "I get it."

"Then tell me," Gill said.

"That guy should've believed it when his friends told him Jesus was alive again," Maggie said. "He shouldn't have made Jesus prove it to him."

"What's that got to do with Sophie being mad at God, though?" Fiona said.

Sophie squirmed. It had felt so good for a moment there, to feel like she was Thomas really seeing Jesus. If only Jesus had stayed in her mind long enough for her to ask him why he seemed so far away lately, why he was giving her so many things to deal with that couldn't be fixed.

"Good question," Dr. Peter said. "If what Maggie just said is true, then Sophie shouldn't have so many doubts."

Sophie felt her eyes start in alarm, but Dr. Peter put his hand up. "It *is* true that we need the kind of faith that believes without seeing. But most of us don't have that right away and all the time, and it's okay."

Maggie looked up from the paper where, as usual, she was taking notes. "It is?"

"Sure. Faith is alive—it's something that grows stronger over time. We grow at different rates too. Don't we all need to see and hear God for *ourselves*?"

As Dr. Peter looked around the room, Sophie stayed very still.

Dr. Peter went on in his it's-going-to-be-all-right voice. "Jesus knew that poor Thomas didn't have a whole lot of imagination. Back at the Last Supper, when Jesus said the disciples knew where he was going and someday they'd join him, Thomas disagreed. He said he personally had no idea where Jesus was going, and he sure didn't know the way to get there."

"He was a bit thick, that one," Darbie said.

Sophie sat up straighter in her beanbag.

"He just took everything very literally," Dr. Peter said.

"Like Maggie," Fiona said. "No offense, Mags."

"No need to be offended." Dr. Peter grinned at Maggie. "Thomas gave Jesus the opportunity to say that *he* was the way. All they had to do was follow Jesus, even if they didn't know where. That's the whole reason we're here studying him, right? So we can follow?"

"But I don't know where he is right now," Sophie said. "Everything is so—wrong."

"I felt that way when I first got leukemia," Kitty said.

Dr. Peter nodded. "But even before you went into remission, God gave you what you needed to get you through."

"But God won't cure my baby sister," Sophie said. "Once you have Down syndrome, you always have it. There's no remission, either."

All eyes were once again on Dr. Peter.

"All I can say, from my own experience," he said in a thick voice, "is that when God isn't giving you what you're asking him for, he usually has something else—something better—in mind."

Something better? Sophie felt like arguing. But she pinched her lips tight. What could be better than Hope being cured of Down syndrome?

Fiona raised one eyebrow. "Didn't Jesus basically tell Thomas he needed to believe without seeing? And we have to too, right?"

"Yes, but there's something else." Dr. Peter scooted to the edge of his beanbag so he could look right into Sophie's eyes. "It's fine—even *good*—to have doubts about what God's doing at certain times. One Christian writer I really like—a man named Frederick Buechner—said, 'Doubts are the ants in the pants of faith.'"

"Ewww!" Willoughby said. The poodle was back.

Dr. Peter grinned. "Just like ants get you moving, doubts keep your faith stirred up and moving."

"I don't like ants," Sophie said. She could almost feel them on her, making her itch, like she'd been doing for days.

"And you don't like doubts, either, do you?" Dr. Peter's voice was soft. "Nobody ever said having faith was always going to be a picnic."

Fiona grinned. "My Boppa always says, 'What's a picnic without ants?'"

Dr. Peter smiled an almost-sad smile at Sophie. "It's okay to ask questions, Loodle. As long as you don't stop trying to find the answers."

Eight

When class was over and Darbie's aunt Emily brought in cheese, crackers, and juice boxes, everyone leaped for them as if big weights had been removed from their shoulders.

Everyone except Sophie. It was true—she didn't feel quite so itchy now. She was just sad. Squeezy cheese from a can wasn't going to cheer her up.

Dr. Peter leaned on the wall next to her. "This is very hard stuff, isn't it, Loodle?"

"I don't know what to do." Sophie shifted her shoulders. "I keep praying and asking ..."

"Why don't you do what you always do? Make a movie."

Sophie pulled her chin in. "We tried to make a movie with Brooke, but it didn't help her. Besides, everybody hated doing it."

"I was thinking of a video record of your baby sister's first weeks. Not a Film Club production—just a Sophie movie."

"How would I do that?" Sophie said. Hope couldn't exactly follow a script.

"Just film her doing her baby-thing." Dr. Peter grinned down at her. "You're not really Thomas—you *do* have an imagination. That makes it easier for you to accept things on faith. I know you will eventually, once you get your questions answered."

The fear fingers took another grab at Sophie's heart. Making a movie was supposed to take her mind *off* things she didn't want to think about.

She shook her head. "I don't really think a movie about Hope will help."

"Aw, Loodle," Dr. Peter said. "I think she's the perfect place to find God's answers."

Sophie wasn't sure about that. But Dr. Peter had never sent her in the wrong direction before. With those icy fingers still trying to get a hold on her, she took out her camera that night after supper and went in search of her baby sister.

Hope was asleep in her crib. Sophie focused on the little face, which was turned to the side as she lay on her back. Sophie thought her eyes looked normal when they were closed. But the little tongue was, as always, poking out from between her lips. She made funny little squeaky sounds as she breathed.

After about a minute, Sophie turned the camera off.

"You need to do something," she whispered to the baby.

"Don't you dare wake her up." Lacie padded across the thick carpet and leaned over the crib to straighten Hope's blanket. "What are you doing, anyway?"

"Making a movie," Sophie said.

"About Hope?" Lacie said.

"Yeah. I think it's gonna be kinda boring."

"You should tell Mama and Daddy you're doing it. They'll be super relieved."

"Why?"

Lacie gave the baby a soft pat before she turned to Sophie, arms folded. "They're worried that you aren't bonding with her. With you making a movie about her, at least they'll stop thinking you're jealous of her or something."

"Jealous?" That was one of the few bad feelings she *didn't* have about Hope.

"You have to admit it's pretty weird," Lacie said. "You were all over Zeke when he was born, but you don't even want to hold Hope."

"I've held her," Sophie said.

Lacie just looked at her.

"I'll take some footage of you covering her up with the blanket and stuff," Sophie said.

As Sophie focused in, Lacie lifted the blanket and let it float back down over baby Hope's little pink self.

"What's that red thing in there?" Sophie said, still filming.

Lacie pulled a plastic figure out from under the blanket. "What else?" she said. "Spider-Man."

Friday, Brooke was back in PE class, and Sophie felt a wave of sadness when she saw her in the locker room. But when the Flakes reported to the gym for roll check, Brooke herself looked pretty happy. The Pops appeared to be teaching her a cheer.

"I haven't seen them do a routine since they got kicked off the squad," Fiona said.

Brooke stood between Cassie and Anne-Stuart. Julia was in front of them, demonstrating a hip swivel. Sophie had definitely never seen Willoughby or any of the other GMMS cheerleaders do that, and Brooke wasn't quite getting the hang of it. She looked like she was stirring a giant pot of sand.

"You have to move your rear end," Cassie said.

"You're doing fine, Brookie," Julia said. "It's the words that are important."

"Brookie?" Fiona said under her breath. "This is definitely suspicious."

Sophie had to agree. Julia was having far too much fun for a jilted ex-cheerleader passing her skills on to a girl with no rhythm and even less coordination. Brooke's hips actually appeared to go in two different directions.

At the blast of Coach Yates's whistle, everyone but Brooke fell into line. She remained with her back to Coach, still swirling her hips.

"If you're not where you're supposed to be when I get there, Singletary," Coach Yates yelled, "I'm counting you absent."

"I'm here!" Brooke yelled back. When she turned to run toward her place, Sophie saw her face for the first time. She had on so much eye shadow, Sophie wasn't sure how she kept her eyelids open.

"Why's she wearing all that makeup?" Maggie said.

"Because we gave her a makeover." Julia flipped her hair over her shoulder. "We're trying to help her fit in."

"You *are*?" Willoughby said. Sophie could see her stifling a shriek.

"*We* aren't a clique," Anne-Stuart said. "*We* try to include new people."

Cassie narrowed her eyes at Sophie. "Not like *some* people we know."

Sophie put her hand on Fiona's shoulder. She could almost hear her best friend's teeth grinding.

When they got to their volleyball court, Coach Yates came over. "Another team is short a person, and they requested you, Brooke." She nodded her too-tight ponytail toward the Pops/Loops court.

Brooke let out a whoop and attempted a cartwheel in that direction. Although it looked more like somebody falling out of bed, the Corn Pops clapped.

"Okay—now I'm not just suspicious," Fiona said to Sophie. "I've moved on to dead certain. Something's going on."

Whatever it was, Sophie watched it continue through the PE period. The Corn Pops adjusted Brooke's braid and redid her lipstick every time the ball went out of bounds. When Tod told her she stunk at volleyball, Julia said it didn't matter because she looked "too cute" on the court. Tod sent a lot of death stares Brooke's way, but Julia shot him down with a few of her own.

"They're setting somebody up for something," Willoughby said. "So everybody watch your back."

Sophie nodded. That was definitely something they didn't have to see to believe.

In the locker room, Brooke dragged her clothes to the Corn Pops' corner, but they dressed her in an outfit they appeared to have brought from home, complete with a skimpy orange shrug that tied in the front and a matching purse with giant sequins on it. To Sophie she looked like a sparkly pumpkin. As Brooke strutted out of the locker room, several sequins fell off and left a trail behind her.

Sophie had a fidgety feeling inside. She really should go after Brooke and tell her the Corn Pops didn't invite girls like her into their group without an evil reason.

But Brooke was surrounded by Pops, smiling like Queen Julia herself. Was Project Brooke over for the Flakes? Sophie wondered. Could anybody ever really save her?

Sophie couldn't answer that question. Not yet, anyway. But Dr. Peter had said not to stop looking for the answers.

At lunch, Darbie had an answer of her own. "Coach Nanini pulled me out of Miss Imes' class to talk to me," she said.

"I saw that," Fiona said. "What'd he say?"

Sophie could see Darbie trying not to smile. "He said he and some of the other teachers talked about it, and they decided Brooke had too many problems for Round Table to handle. He tried to get her some special help, but he said she won't take it. It's like she won't admit she has ADHD or anything else. Anyway, I'm off the hook."

Fiona looked at Sophie. "So that means we're *all* off the hook."

"Seriously, Sophie," Darbie said. "If Brooke doesn't want help, what are we supposed to do?"

"I guess you're right," Sophie said.

But she was squirmy inside again. As she tore her sandwich into tiny pieces, Dr. Peter's words came back to her: *Doubts are the ants in the pants of faith.* Just like annoying little ants got you moving, itchy doubts kept your faith stirred up and moving.

After school, Sophie picked up her camera from Mr. Stires' storage room. If she intended to keep asking questions, then she'd better keep looking for answers—and be ready to record them.

Saturday morning, she took more footage of Hope sleeping, sometimes on her side, sometimes on her back. Sophie decided babies must sleep a lot because they couldn't do much of anything else. Especially this baby.

It surprised her then, when she was filming Mama feeding her a bottle Saturday afternoon, that Hope found Mama's finger with her tiny ones and wrapped them around it.

"I didn't know she could do that!" Sophie said.

"Isn't it the cutest?" Mama leaned down and kissed the miniature fingers. Baby Hope still held on.

Sophie zoomed in. It was like Hope knew that was Mama and she wasn't letting go for anything. Could that be?

"Come here, Soph," Mama said.

Sophie put the camera in one hand and sat next to her. Mama pulled her finger away from the baby.

"Just put your pinky right in her palm," she said. "Watch what happens."

Moving in slow motion, Sophie placed her little finger against Hope's soft, warm hand. In an instant, Hope was clinging to Sophie. Almost as if she trusted her.

"This is your big sister," Mama cooed to her.

Hope stopped sucking on the bottle and moved her eyes. They stopped as if she was looking right at Mama.

"Hello," Mama said in her softest wisp of a voice. "Is that my Baby Doll?"

"Does she know you?" Sophie said.

"She does." Mama laughed, a little tinkle bell of a laugh. "Of course, we've been together a long time. You keep talking to her, and she'll know your voice too."

"Are you sure?" Sophie said.

"Very sure." Mama looked straight at her. "Sophie, she's a person, just like the rest of us."

Sophie knew her face was turning as red as Nathan's. Mama went back to cooing at Hope, and Sophie went back to filming. Inside, though, she felt something go soft.

While she took movies all weekend, Sophie discovered that Hope turned her head toward Lacie's voice too, and that Zeke's seemed to be her favorite finger to latch onto. He got her to curl her hand around a Spider-Man figure's leg, but Daddy took it away from her.

"You don't know where this thing has been, Little Rookie," he said to her. "I'm afraid to find that out myself."

The filming also showed Sophie that nobody had more fun with baby Hope than Daddy. The best shots she took were of the two of them. He walked around with her tucked into the crook of his arm, kind of like a football, and talked to her as if she could understand everything he said.

Sophie was in Hope's nursery Sunday afternoon, filming Daddy changing her diaper, when something crashed in the direction of Zeke's room.

"Want me to check that out?" Sophie said.

"I'll do it," Daddy said. "If he's halfway up the wall, you won't be able to get him down anyway."

"What about Hope?" Sophie nodded toward the half-dressed baby on the changing table.

"Don't let her fall off. I'll be right back."

"But how do I ..." Her question faded as Daddy made a hasty exit. Sophie looked down at Hope. She lay very still, with only the occasional hand or foot popping up. It was so quiet in the nursery that Sophie could hear her tiny breaths.

This was the first time she'd been alone with her when she was awake. The fear fingers curled around Sophie's heart the way Hope's fingers curled around somebody's pinky. Only these squeezed hard. *What do I do if she starts crying?*

Baby Hope jerked as if she'd read Sophie's mind. Her eyes searched the ceiling, and her arms flailed at her sides. The telltale crumple wrinkled her brow.

"Don't cry," Sophie said. "Come on, don't cry. I don't know what to do if you cry."

Hope let out a frightened squawk and turned her head to the side.

"Don't fall off," Sophie said, leaning her stomach against the changing table.

A mind-flash of her baby sister tumbling to the floor almost blinded her. Sophie scooped the tiny body up in her arms and held her against her chest.

"Don't cry," Sophie whispered to her. "I would never let you fall."

Hope stopped wiggling. The next squawk settled into a sigh, and she breathed tiny whisper breaths against Sophie's neck. Sophie closed her eyes, but she couldn't imagine anything. She could only be right there, holding her baby sister.

"Looks like you two are getting along pretty well," Daddy said from the doorway.

"You should take her." Sophie pressed against her father until he took the baby from her.

Then she fled to her room on the edge of tears. The thing she'd feared all along had happened. She'd started to love a sister who would never be okay.

Nine

The ants-in-the-pants feeling kept Sophie's mind itching until Monday morning. No answers yet, but Dr. Peter had said to keep asking.

So she took the camera to school, just in case, and went to Mr. Stires' room to put it away before first period. The storage room wasn't open yet. He was still in his puffy down jacket, pulling at his mustache as he listened to Julia Cummings, who had her back to the door. Sophie didn't have to see her face to know it was her so-sweet-it's-disgusting voice.

"I'm not trying to get her in trouble," Julia said. "I just wish you'd talk to her before we have our next lab. I don't want to end up with some other animal's insides on me—"

Julia stopped as Mr. Stires' eyes flickered toward Sophie. When Julia glanced over her shoulder, Sophie had the strange sensation that Julia had already known Sophie was there.

"Just leave the camera on the desk, Sophie," Mr. Stires said. "I'll put it away."

Sophie did. As she turned to leave, she caught a satisfied smirk on Julia's face.

"Why is she just now tattling to Mr. Stires about the lizard brain?" Fiona said when Sophie told the Corn Flakes in the gym. "If she wanted to get you in trouble, she would have said something to him right away."

Darbie gave an elaborate sigh. "We always have to have drama. We just get done with Brooke, and now we have the Pops again."

"Oh — my — gosh," Kitty said.

Sophie turned in time to see Brooke bound into the gym wearing Pepto-Bismol-pink tennis shoes and neon-purple track pants with matching jacket.

"Those are Cassie's shoes," Willoughby whispered.

Kitty nodded. "And I've seen Anne-Stuart wear that work-out suit."

Fiona pushed the stubborn strip of hair away from her eye. "But Anne-Stuart didn't accessorize with a boa."

Sophie stared as Brooke pulled a lime green string of feathers out of the jacket.

"Just what do you intend to do with that?" Coach Yates, of course, yelled. Her face looked double-pinched.

"It's for my ch — "

"It's mine." Julia flashed Coach Yates a plastic smile. "I'm letting her use it." She turned oh-so-sweetly to Brooke. "I didn't mean for you to bring it to class. That's for later." And then she winked.

"A wink is not good," Willoughby told the Corn Flakes when they were gathered on their court. "In Corn Pop world, that means something is their little secret."

"An evil secret," Kitty put in.

"Don't let's be doddering on about that now," Darbie said. "She's not our responsibility anymore."

Sophie felt a pang as she caught the ball Jimmy tossed to her and headed for the serving position.

"Sophie," Fiona whispered from outside the court where she was waiting to rotate in.

"What?" Sophie said.

"You're not going to leave it alone, are you?"

"Leave what alone?"

"Brooke—and the Corn Pops."

"You're supposed to serve now," Maggie called from the net.

Sophie held the ball in one hand and swung the other arm back.

"Okay." Fiona sighed. "Find out what you can. I'll cover for you."

Sophie popped the ball up with her fist. She didn't care if it went over the net. Fiona had given her the first reason to smile in a long time. Maybe this was a little bit of an answer.

After class, Fiona walked backward in front of the rest of the Corn Flakes, chattering away about some complicated vocabulary word they just *had* to know. Sophie dawdled by the ball basket until Cassie and Brooke passed through the doorway and headed for the locker room, heads bent together. Cassie was whispering, but Sophie knew Brooke's version of a whisper could be heard from a hundred paces. Sophie gave them about ten and followed, ears perked up.

Cassie sounded like she was saying, *Mutter mutter mutter mutter.*

Brooke said, "I haven't had a chance yet."

"Mutter mutter mutter," said Cassie.

She put her arm around Brooke and pulled her closer, so that Sophie couldn't even hear her muttering.

"Wicked!" Brooke said.

They turned into the locker room with Sophie behind them. She hurried so she wouldn't lose them at the next turn past the showers. When she rounded the corner, only Cassie was standing there with her back to Sophie, blocking her way.

"Um, excuse me," Sophie said.

Cassie didn't answer or budge.

Sophie tried to get past her, but Cassie moved with her. When Sophie jockeyed the other way, Cassie was right there.

"Could I please get by?" Sophie said.

Cassie looked over her shoulder. "Oh, sorry." Her voice had as much expression as the recorded lady on voice mail. "I didn't see you there."

"So—could I get by?" Sophie said.

"Sure."

Cassie stepped aside so Sophie could pass between her and the row of shower stalls. But Sophie didn't get a foot farther before someone grabbed her arm and yanked her behind the first curtain.

"Hope you like cold water!" Brooke said.

The faucet squeaked on, Brooke leaped out of the stall, and Sophie was soaked by liquid ice cubes. Gasping and groping, she finally threw herself out through the shower curtain. Cassie and Brooke were nowhere to be seen.

Shivering right down to her bones, Sophie sloshed down the hall, clothes dripping near-icicles on the floor. Ahead of her, damp footprints led not to the locker area, but in the other direction, straight to a door marked SUPPLIES.

"You always leave a trail, Brooke," Sophie said out loud. She pushed the door open and slipped inside.

It was dark, but Sophie found a switch on the wall and lit up the storage room. Brooke was hidden from the knees up behind an open shelf unit full of paper towels and toilet tissue. At the bottom, though, were a pair of Pepto-Bismol-pink tennis shoes and two legs clad in neon purple.

"I see you, Brooke," Sophie said. "You might as well come out."

"I don't got nothing to say to you."

90

Sophie rolled her eyes. When did Brooke *not* have anything to say?

"All I want to know is why you pushed me into the shower," Sophie said. "I'm freezing."

"Serves you right. You're just a troublemaker."

"Me?" Sophie's voice squeaked upward.

"Don't play innocent." Brooke's pink shoes shuffled. "I know about you."

"Know what?"

"You're the one who made all of Julia's and Anne-Stuart's friends hate them."

"What are you—"

"You're the one who made Tod Ravelli hate *me*."

Sophie stopped interrupting. The girl who didn't have anything to say was on a roll.

"You're the one who got me suspended too," Brooke said. "Since you're all buddy-buddy with Coach Ninooni—or whatever his name is."

Sophie wrapped her arms around her shivering self, but she was hot on the inside. The Corn Pops had been at work on Brooke, but there was no way to prove it. If she let Brooke talk long enough, she'd probably spill it, but what good would that do? It would be Brooke's word against the Pops', and Brooke hadn't exactly built a reputation for being trustworthy.

But something tripped up that thought. Getting the Pops in trouble wasn't what mattered. It was keeping Brooke *out* of trouble.

"I don't know why you had to do all that stuff to me." There was a quiver in Brooke's voice. "I thought you were my friend—putting me in that movie and everything."

"I was *trying* to be your friend," Sophie said.

91

"No, you weren't!" The metal shelf unit shook, and a roll of toilet paper tumbled to the floor.

"Would you come out of there before everything falls off?" Sophie said.

"No." Brooke's voice twisted, as if that was the only way she could keep back tears. "I hate you. All I was to you was Project Brooke. My *friends* showed me."

Sophie felt as if she'd just been slapped—and that she deserved it.

In the silence, Coach Yates could be heard down the hall, yelling, "Who left this shower on?"

Brooke stumbled out from behind the shelves, face blotchy. The ends of the green feather boa hung forlornly from the bottom of the purple jacket, and one sleeve was wet. "Are you gonna tell on me?" she said.

Sophie closed her eyes. *Brooke didn't even think about that before she dragged me into the shower.*

"All right," Coach Yates yelled, "you have two minutes before the bell rings."

Brooke looked wildly around the supply room like she was searching for an escape hatch. Sophie's heart pounded. This might as well be happening to her.

After all, she thought, it's my fault. I have to at least try to fix it.

But her "helping" had messed things up before, and Sophie knew it. She'd wanted to fix Brooke and she'd just made her hate the Flakes instead.

Just keep asking the questions. Wasn't that what Dr. Peter had said?

Which way do I go? she prayed to eyes she couldn't see.

"One minute!" Coach Yates yelled.

Her voice was getting farther away. Brooke wedged herself between Sophie and the door.

"They said you'd tell on me, but they'll swear I never came near you—"

"I won't tell, Brooke," Sophie said, "if you'll give me one more chance to help you."

"Help me with what? I'm just fine the way I am—my friends say so."

Sophie pulled her chin in. "Julia and them?"

"Yes—*they* really like me—*they* don't try to change me!"

Before Sophie could point out that the Corn Pops had all but done plastic surgery on her, Brooke shoved her aside and flew out of the room.

Sophie felt like a soggy, shivering lump of failure as she dragged herself out too. When she turned the corner toward the now-empty locker area, she ran into Coach Yates (as Fiona would say) "literally."

Coach Yates looked from Sophie's drenched clothes to the front of her own sweatshirt, now bearing a wet Sophie-print.

"What in the world happened to you, LaCroix?"

"Um, I was in the shower," Sophie said.

"With your clothes on?"

Sophie could only nod.

Coach Yates put up her hand. "I don't even want to know. You have fifteen seconds to get dressed."

Sophie was cold and deflated when she got to Miss Imes' classroom. Julia and Anne-Stuart were just inside the door, and they both spattered laughter into their hands at the same moment. From the glow in their eyes, Sophie figured Brooke had completed her assigned task even more successfully than they could have imagined.

But, then, they never did have much imagination, Sophie thought. Fiona and Darbie, on the other hand, were gaping at her like they were dreaming up the worst.

Before she could get to them, Miss Imes said, "Bad time of year to be walking around with wet hair, Sophie."

"Sorry," Sophie said.

Miss Imes' eyebrows pointed up. "Sorry for what?"

For everything, Sophie thought. She slunk to her desk, slid into her seat, and closed her eyes. She even put her hands over her glasses. But she could still hear the twist of hurt in Brooke's voice when she said, *I hate you. All I was to you was Project Brooke.* There was definitely no room in Sophie's mind-picture for Jesus.

But somehow she had to believe he was there. *I'm trying really hard to follow you,* she prayed silently, *but would you please show me where we're going?*

When Sophie looked up, Fiona was giving her a bug-eyed stare and pointing to her hair as if to say, *What's with the wet head?*

There was no way to communicate back — not with Miss Imes gazing pointedly in every direction. But seeing Fiona made Sophie think of something. As she scribbled down the problems from the board, her mind raced.

How did Brooke find out the Flakes referred to her as Project Brooke?

Sophie glanced at Julia and Anne-Stuart, who were calculating away with their sharpened pencils as if math were their sole purpose in life. Brooke said her "friends" had told her — people who "really liked her" and "didn't try to change her." Sophie gnawed on her stubby pencil. It was crystal clear to her that the Corn Pops *didn't* like Brooke, and that they *were* trying to change her — and using her in the process.

And then Sophie took in a huge breath that threatened to drag her eraser down her windpipe.

The Corn Flakes don't like Brooke, either. And Brooke was right. All we did was try to change her.

"Miss Imes?" Julia said, in a voice as sweet as pancake syrup. "Would you show me how to do number five? I know you explained it, but I need you to show me."

Sophie eyes sprang open.

Show me. I need you to show me.

Brooke hadn't said, "My friends *told* me." Sophie could almost hear her quivery voice again in her mind. She'd said, "My friends *showed* me."

But what did they show her that actually said the words *Project Brooke*? Where was it ever written down? At the risk of being pierced by Miss Imes' pointy look, Sophie scanned the room.

Vincent? No, he and Darbie were always behind the camera.

Fiona? She never wrote anything down. She just dictated to Maggie, who recorded *everything*—even stuff that didn't have anything to do with the movie.

Sophie's pencil fell out of her hand, and she didn't bother to pick it up. She closed her eyes and heard Darbie say, *Brooke's always going through everybody's belongings.*

Sophie watched the clock, fear fingers squeezing the breath out of her. Five long minutes until the bell rang for lunch. An eternity before she'd be able to get to Maggie.

Ten

When the bell finally ended math class, Sophie told Fiona and Darbie everything as they sailed to their lockers.

"So you think Brooke saw the words *Project Brooke* written in our Treasure Book?" Fiona said.

"How could she?" Darbie said. "Maggie would never let her near it."

Sophie talked over her shoulder as she took the last turn into the locker hall. Fiona and Darbie practically ran to keep up. "Brooke said Julia and them *showed* her."

"So you think one of the *Pops* saw it in the Treasure Book?" Fiona said.

Darbie scowled. "How? You know Maggie wouldn't let one of them get a *sniff* of it."

"I don't have the answers." Sophie shook her head. "We don't even know if Maggie wrote it down in there. We just have to ask her."

Maggie, Willoughby, and Kitty were already at their lockers when Sophie squealed her tennis shoes around the end of the row. She took the last few steps in one leap.

"You're not supposed to run in the halls," Maggie said. "You could get in trouble—"

"Maggie!" Sophie said. "Did you ever write the words *Project Brooke* in the Treasure Book?"

Maggie blinked. "I wrote everything down."

Fiona stuck her head between them. "But did you write down those exact words: *Project Brooke*?"

"Yikes, Fiona," Willoughby said. "Why are you all up in Maggie's dentalwork?"

Fiona pointed to Maggie's backpack. "Could you just look?"

Maggie squatted and unzipped her pack, which was on the floor. She grew as still as a stump.

"Isn't it in there?" Fiona said.

"It's in here. Just not in the place I always keep it."

Sophie's heart nearly stopped as Maggie held up the Treasure Book. Or, at least, what was left of it. Its former shiny purple cover was all jagged strips that hung from the binding like a tattered flag. Some of the cuts dug deep into the pages.

"How long has it been like *that*, Mags?" Fiona asked.

"I didn't know it *was* like that!"

Sophie knelt beside Maggie. "How did somebody get in your backpack?"

"Or did you leave the book out someplace?" Kitty said.

"I never do that!" Willoughby said, "Well, then *somebody* got into your backpack *somehow*—"

Sophie put her hands over her ears. "Stop!"

The Corn Flakes froze as one.

"Sorry, Mags," Fiona said. "It's not your fault."

The bell rang, and Darbie shooed them all toward the cafeteria, explaining to Kitty, Willoughby, and Maggie what Brooke had said to Sophie in the supply closet.

Maggie trudged next to Sophie, hugging her bag to her chest. She didn't utter so much as a grunt even when they were all settled at the table. Nobody opened a lunch. Sophie thought she might be sick.

"Fiona is right, Mags," Sophie said. "It's not your fault. It's mine for ever thinking of doing that stupid movie in the first place."

"No, it's mine," Fiona said. "I named it Project Brooke. That was *so* un-Corn Flake."

"It's mine for even writing it down," Maggie muttered.

"Maybe you didn't." Kitty looked doubtfully at what used to be the Treasure Book. "'Course, there's no way to tell now."

Fiona nodded. "I looked. When you push the strips together, you can see it: 'Project Brooke.'"

"I'd like to say something." Darbie jammed her hair behind her ears. "It isn't any of *our* faults that somebody got into our private property and cut it all in flitters."

"*Somebody?*" Willoughby said. "We know it was Brooke."

Fiona nodded. "We just don't know how and when."

"But we know why." Sophie's voice squeaked like a clarinet some beginner student couldn't play.

"Who cares why?" Maggie said. "She broke a rule, and she has to take the consequences."

"That's right." Darbie looked right at Sophie. "I hope you don't think we should let this go just because we feel bad that we hurt Brooke's feelings."

Sophie looked miserably at the Treasure Book. Maggie was smoothing down its hopeless cover, as if she could make it whole again.

"The Corn Pops told her a bunch of lies," Sophie said. "And I bet when she saw this she just got mad like she does." Sophie looked again at the book that had held so many of their dreams. "I want to try to help her one more time. Let's just give it another day."

"Why?" Darbie said. "I'm about to eat the head off somebody, but you don't see me looking for Brooke so I can reef her."

"You don't have to," Willoughby whispered. "'Cause here she comes."

Kitty whimpered and hid her face behind Maggie's shoulder. Sophie slid the Treasure Book into her lap under the table, just as Brooke arrived.

"Oh, my — what's this show?" Darbie muttered.

Brooke was still in Anne-Stuart's purple track outfit, but she'd had some other changes made since Sophie last saw her.

Her red hair was in a folded ponytail on top of her head, held in place by a blue-sequined scrunchie. Sophie was sure someone had applied makeup to her face with a spatula, especially the lipstick. There appeared to be an entire tube of Shimmering Cherry on her lips. The effect of clown-at-a-fashion-show was completed with the green feather boa Brooke had draped over her shoulders and wrapped around each arm like stripes on barber poles.

"Hi, Brooke." Willoughby wore her automatic cheerleader smile. "You look — "

"Interesting!" Sophie said. "Don't you guys think she looks interesting?"

"Fascinating," Fiona said.

Kitty pulled out the cereal box. "Want some Cheerios?"

Brooke only looked over her shoulder. Then she straightened up and closed her eyes for a second, as if she were concentrating.

"Are you okay?" Sophie said.

Brooke slapped her hands together and threw her arms over her head, green feathers and all. She looked like a parrot trying out for cheerleading.

"Ready?" she shouted. "Okay! Give me an *F* !"

Nobody answered so she answered herself and went on with, "Give me an *L*!"

"This is embarrassing," Kitty whispered to Sophie.

But Sophie said, "*L*."

Brooke flung her arms into a point over her head. "Now give me an *A*!"

"Come on, you guys," Sophie said through gritted teeth. "*A*!"

The arms took a flying turn to the side. "Give me a *K* !"

"*K*!" Sophie said. Kitty and Willoughby joined in feebly.

Face now as red as Nathan's had ever gotten, Brooke screamed, "Give me an—" She paused, made-up brow furrowing like a wad of clay. "Oh—give me an *E*!"

"*E*!" cried half the cafeteria.

"Sophie, stop!" Fiona hissed at her. "Don't you hear what she's spelling?"

"Give—me—an—*S*!"

Sophie saw the word in her head, where she'd pictured it hundreds of special times. She went cold.

"What do we have?" Brooke yelled.

There was a slight pause.

"What *do* we have?" Gill the Wheatie said at the other end of the table.

"Flakes?" said Vincent across the aisle.

Willoughby plastered her hands over her mouth. The other Corn Flakes looked too stunned to move.

"Flakes!" Brooke swiveled her hips in a clumsy circle. "Coooorn Flakes! That's what they call themselves!" Plunging toward the table end, she straightened her arms, grabbed on, and stuck out both legs to the sides.

"Don't, Brooke!" Willoughby cried. "You won't make it!"

Brooke didn't. What looked like an attempt to land a pike on top of the table ended in Brooke halfway *under* the table on her hind end. But she wasn't finished. She scrambled up, amid screaming middle-school laughter, and hoisted herself onto her knees on the table. With her hands cupped around her mouth, she shouted, "These are the Corn Flakes!"

"The what?" somebody shouted back.

The noise died down a level. Brooke pointed at Sophie's head, and then Fiona's. Sophie was sure she was going to throw up, right there. Beside her, Fiona was as stiff as a pole.

"They call themselves the Corn Flakes," Brooke cried. "That's because they *are* flakes. A clique full of flakes. Don't ever be their friend because you can't trust them."

Gill and Harley both stood up, and some of the other Wheaties too. "That's not true!" one of them said.

"I trust them," Jimmy said. Nathan nodded, face the color of a match head.

Vincent got to his feet. "Where did you get this information? Sounds like you made it up to me."

"No." Brooke pulled the back of her hand, still clad in green feathers, across her lips. Titters erupted from the crowd as she wiped lipstick from mouth to ear. "I'm not making it up. I got the 411 from my friends, who are *not* flakes, even though *these* flakes have wrecked everything for them."

She flung a hand toward Sophie's Corn Flakes, whose faces were frozen into portraits of shock.

"Name your source," Vincent said to Brooke.

"Huh?" Brooke said.

"Who told you?"

"They're right over—" Brooke jabbed a finger toward the Pops' table. It was empty. Not even Tod and Colton were there. The feather boa slid off one arm. "They *were* over there," Brooke said. "It's Jul—"

"Brooke, get down," Sophie said.

As the cafeteria buzzed around them, Darbie thawed from her frozen state and grabbed one of Brooke's arms. Fiona took the other. Brooke stared at them and then at herself, as if she'd just noticed she was on top of the table.

Darbie and Fiona hauled her into a chair. With lipstick smeared across her face and sweat making streams through the makeup, Brooke looked like a little girl who'd just been caught in her mother's cosmetics.

She really is a little girl, Sophie thought. It took away some of her urge to stuff the feather boa down Brooke's throat. While Darbie muttered and Fiona gritted her teeth and Kitty whined into Maggie's unmoving shoulder, Sophie watched Brooke crane her neck toward the cafeteria door. She looked desperate, as if that same little girl had completely *lost* her mother.

"Who are you looking for?" Sophie said.

"My friends."

Darbie snorted. "You mean the *friends* that took off and left you making an eejit of yourself?"

Brooke came halfway off the seat, but Sophie grabbed her arm.

"Did your, um, friends tell you we called ourselves the Corn Flakes?" Sophie said.

"No. I read it." Brooke looked as if she wanted to bite her tongue off when Maggie pulled the mangled Treasure Book from Sophie's lap and laid it on the table.

"Did you read it in here?" Maggie said.

Sophie could almost see the possible lies flipping through Brooke's mind. Again she half rose from the seat and threw glances at every corner of the room.

"Okay," Fiona said, "let me just tell you what probably happened, and you can tell me if I'm right."

Darbie and Maggie wore matching scowls, but Sophie said, "Good idea."

Brooke lowered herself back into the seat and stared down at the Treasure Book.

Fiona folded her hands on the table. "When we were making the movie, the Po—uh, Julia and your other *friends* asked you if you'd ever seen inside our book. You said no, and they said if you looked in it, you'd find out what we were *really* like." Fiona brushed her hair aside. "How am I doing so far?"

"That's *maybe* what happened." Brooke wrapped the end of the boa around her finger, so that it too was coated with lipstick.

"So," Fiona went on, "you got into Maggie's backpack, sometime when she wasn't looking, and you found the book. When you saw that we called the movie Project Brooke, you were incensed, and you stabbed it multiple times with—something."

"I didn't use incense," Brooke said.

"No," Sophie said. "She means you got mad."

"And then you went back and told your *friends*." Fiona made quotation marks with her fingers. "And you also told them that the book said we were the Corn Flakes."

Willoughby's curls bounced. "So they taught you a cheer about Corn Flakes. They dressed you up like Ronald McDonald and told you to do the cheer in front of everybody."

Brooke looked at Sophie. "You all make it sound like they were trying to make me look stupid."

"No," Sophie said. "They were using you to make *us* look stupid."

"Because if they'd done it themselves," Maggie said, "they'd get in trouble."

"But they're nice! They let me wear their clothes—they wanted me on their team."

Fiona leaned toward her. "And where are they now?"

"They'll be back."

"No, they won't." Kitty looked at Brooke from over Maggie's shoulder. "I used to be in their group, and all they did was use me too."

"Me, three," Willoughby said.

"Personally, I think they even use each other." Fiona sat back, arms folded. "You can believe them if you want to, but it's only going to get worse if you do."

"*Don't* believe Julia and the rest of them, Brooke," Sophie said. "I mean it. We were wrong before when we made you our project, but we honestly wanted to help you because—"

"Because I mess everything up." Brooke wound the boa around her neck. "Everybody tells me that all the time."

"We were trying to help you *not* mess things up, only we did it the wrong way. We're sorry." Sophie glanced around the table at the friends who suddenly wouldn't look at her. "Well, *I'm* sorry, anyway."

The rest of the Corn Flakes were quiet for the longest minute Sophie had ever lived. Questions in her own mind tortured her.

What if nobody had learned anything? What if the Corn Flakes really were nothing but a clique? If they abandoned Brooke now, were they really any better than the Corn Pops?

Sophie was so afraid of the answers, she almost ran from them, right out the door.

Brooke pointed at the Treasure Book. "What about that?"

"You mean, are we gonna turn you in?" Willoughby said.

Maggie cradled the book in her hands. "You can't just go around tearing people's stuff up because you get your feelings hurt."

"I don't know how come I did it." Brooke tightened the boa. "I just do stuff, and I don't even know why."

"That's why we were trying to help you," Sophie said. "And we—well, I—still will."

The Corn Flakes still wouldn't look at Sophie, but Brooke did. For a second, she reminded Sophie of baby Hope turning her head toward a voice, like maybe—just *maybe*—she could trust it.

So—is this the Jesus-way? Sophie wondered. It sure looked like it.

But Brooke's eyes sprang open as if some sudden thought terrified her.

"You won't help me!" Brooke cried. "You won't help me when you find out!"

She bolted from the seat, and feet pounded toward the door. The feather boa trailed behind her.

Eleven

The bell rang, and the cafeteria erupted in one big push toward the door. Sophie sank back into her chair.

"What's wrong, Corn Flake?" some kid said to her as he pointed to her still-wet hair. "Too soggy to move?"

For a moment, Sophie had forgotten that Brooke had just told the middle-school world their secret name. She sagged—sogged—further into the seat.

"Like he even knows what a Corn Flake really is," Fiona said. She nudged Sophie to a standing position.

"Do *we*?" Sophie said.

"Do we what?"

"Know what a Corn Flake is?"

Willoughby looped her arm through Sophie's on the other side and tugged her along behind the crowd going out the door.

"We know what it isn't," Darbie said.

Sophie knew she was talking about Brooke and the Pops, but she didn't feel much different from any of them as she trudged toward Mr. Stires' classroom. She tried to ignore the stares of people who stopped whispering as she, Fiona, and Darbie went by.

Mr. Stires stopped them in the doorway. For a minute, Sophie thought he was going to confront her about the lizard brain in Julia's hair. But his face was as cheerful as always.

"How's that film coming along?" he said.

You mean that heinous piece of trash that ruined everything? Sophie wanted to say.

"Uh, we still have a lot of editing to do," Fiona said.

Mr. Stires bobbed his head. "Why don't I take a look at what you have while you're in groups today?"

Sophie felt numb as she nodded. "I'll get it. It's in my camera bag."

She didn't even look at Julia and Anne-Stuart as she headed for the storage room, but she could feel their victory smiles. She was just too tired to care.

The bag was on a shelf above its usual place, and Sophie had to stand on tiptoe to pull it down. Maybe they wouldn't even do any more films, she thought as she grabbed the strap. Maybe everything was just going to be different from now on—

Her thoughts tripped themselves to a stop as the bag fell into her hands. It rattled. It had never rattled before. It wasn't *supposed* to rattle.

The old fear fingers gripped Sophie's heart as she set the bag on a low shelf and squatted to open it. Something was wrong. Way wrong.

Hands sweaty, Sophie unzipped the cover and peered inside. All she saw were broken pieces of what used to be her video camera.

"Hey, Soph," Fiona said from the doorway. "What's taking so long? Mr. Stires is putting us in groups."

"It's ruined," Sophie said. Her voice sounded as wooden as Maggie's.

"No, it's not," Fiona said. "He'll probably put us in the same group."

Sophie didn't answer. She just pointed into the bag as Fiona crossed the storage room. When she looked in, her magic-gray eyes went wide, as if she were staring into headlights.

"It's been pulverized," she said.

If that meant the keeper of their many dreams was now reduced to shards of glass and pieces of bashed-in metal, Fiona was right. Sophie was sure her heart had stopped beating.

"Mr. Stires said to hurry up," said another voice from the doorway. "Why are you foostering—" Darbie took a sharp intake of breath. "What's wrong?" She too gasped into the camera bag. Then she said, "Brooke again."

Sophie couldn't argue with her. Who else was angry enough to smash up the thing that was most important to the girls who made her feel like a project?

Who else indeed? Because as Sophie gazed down into the bag in disbelief, she saw something shiny that wasn't a hunk of camera lens. It looked like the sparkly head of a cat.

"Julia's nail file," she said out loud.

"Where?" Fiona said.

"Right there." Sophie pushed aside some of what was now junk with her finger. The cat on Julia's fancy file seemed to give her an evil smile.

"I don't get it," Fiona said.

"Last call for groups," Mr. Stires called from the classroom.

Sophie slapped the top closed and zipped the zipper.

"What are you doing, Sophie?" Darbie said. "We can't let this go. We have to tell!"

"No," Sophie said. "Brooke has to tell. And first she has to tell me."

"What are you talking about?" Darbie said.

Sophie pulled the memory stick out of the front pocket and slung the rattling camera bag over her shoulder by the strap. "I don't care if everybody thinks the Corn Flakes are a stupid clique. I'm still going to be one, even if I have to do it by myself."

"Who said anything about us not being Corn Flakes anymore?" Fiona's face was the color of Cream of Wheat.

"Nobody said *anything*," Sophie said. "That's just it. At lunch just now, nobody said a word about helping her take back her power from the Corn Pops. Everybody just stood there until she ran off."

"All right, ladies," Mr. Stires said from the doorway. "Darbie, you and Fiona are a group. Sophie, I put you with Jimmy. You have the memory stick so I can look at your film?"

Sophie handed it to him and brushed past Darbie and Fiona to a seat next to Jimmy.

"You okay?" Jimmy's blue eyes were so kind Sophie almost cried—except there was no time for tears.

"No," Sophie said.

"I'm sorry about what Brooke did. I think Corn Flakes is a cool name."

Sophie winced.

"I get it if you don't feel like working right now," Jimmy said. "I'll just do part of the assignment, and you can do the rest for homework."

She nodded. She even wanted to tell him about the camera and ask him to help her make some kind of plan for Brooke. But she just couldn't. This was a Corn Flake problem. Even if she was the only Flake who knew it.

While Jimmy worked, Sophie tried to write down what to do next. She didn't get much further than, *Go to Brooke's tutoring room after school.*

But Fiona and Darbie obviously made more progress. They were waiting for her outside when she left fifth period, and they flanked her as they pulled her down the hall. Sophie could almost see idea light bulbs popping over their heads.

"We didn't get any work done," Fiona said.

"But we weren't foostering about," Darbie said. "We might have a plan."

Sophie stopped just short of their sixth-period classroom. "You changed your minds about helping Brooke?"

"Here's the deal," Fiona said. "Now that everybody on the entire planet knows we call ourselves the Corn Flakes, we can really show them what that means."

"That we aren't some clique," Darbie said. "That we help people take back their power to be who they really are—just like we do for ourselves."

Sophie looked from one of them to the other. They weren't watching her like they were waiting for her to tell them what to do. They looked like they already knew.

"Don't you want to know how we came up with that?" Fiona said.

Without waiting for Sophie to answer, Darbie said, "We did just what you always do. We imagined Jesus."

When Maggie, Willoughby, and Kitty arrived, they gathered in the back of the art room while a substitute teacher wrote her name and THIS IS A STUDY PERIOD on the chalkboard.

"Yikes," Fiona said, "that Jesus-thing works faster than I thought."

They spent the period with their heads bent together, bringing Maggie and the others up to date and wrestling a plan into place. A Jesus-way, they named it.

A few times they all looked at Sophie, as if waiting for her to tell them the right thing to do. But it didn't make her itchy anymore. She knew without seeing that inside each of them there was a little doubt, a little fear, a little being smart about things, a little love. No, a *lot* of love. The things that made them all Corn Flakes.

"Okay," Maggie said when the bell rang. "We have until the late bus to make this happen, right?"

"If we don't, we go to Coach Nanini with the camera first thing tomorrow," Darbie said.

"Whatever happens," Sophie said, "we'll know we did it the Jesus-way."

After a big Corn Flake hug, they split up to go to their stations.

Sophie looked at her watch every five feet as she headed for the Special Ed hall. Like that would make time slow down, she thought. She wished she'd pushed Maggie a little on the deadline. But they had to do it the Jesus-way.

Still, every "What if . . . ?" from *What if Brooke didn't go to her tutoring session today?* to *What if she tied herself up with that stupid boa?* went through Sophie's head until she reached Brooke's classroom door.

She stood on tiptoe to see through the little window. Before she could even get her nose to the glass, the door opened. Sophie stumbled in, straight into Brooke.

They stared at each other long enough for Sophie to see that Brooke had attempted to undo the makeup job. The lipstick and eye shadow had been pushed to the sides of her face along with raised rows of foundation makeup. It looked to Sophie as if a mask had been partly peeled back to reveal the real Brooke.

And the real Brooke looked as if she were staring straight into the face of Godzilla. Sophie took advantage of the frozen moment to pull the camera bag from behind her back and hold it in front of her.

"We need to talk," Sophie said.

Brooke shook her head. "I knew you wouldn't help me when you found out." Then she looked as if she wanted to chomp her tongue off.

Sophie just nodded. "We already figured out you did it. But we don't think you did it alone."

Sophie slipped her hand into the outside pocket of the camera bag and pulled out Julia's nail file. Brooke went so pale that every freckle stood out from her face. She grabbed for the file, but Sophie slid it back into the pocket and pulled her out into the hall.

"Let's talk right here," she said. That had been Darbie's idea. She said if Sophie tried to take Brooke too far, she would make a getaway. If she did try, Sophie knew the next step in the plan. She just hoped Willoughby remembered.

Brooke stood against the wall, kicking at it with her heel while she stared at the camera bag. "I have to give that nail file back to Julia," she said. "I thought I lost it, and she said I was gonna have to pay for it."

"Did you sort of *borrow* it from her?" Sophie said.

"I didn't swipe it! She told me to use it to open your camera and mess with stuff so it wouldn't work. Only first I read that thing about me being a project and how dumb you thought I was." She switched heels. "I was still so mad when Julia got me the camera, and then I couldn't get it open. So I just jumped up and down on it until I heard that teacher with the mustache coming. I guess I left the nail file in there on accident."

Sophie sucked in a huge breath. With a picture in her mind of Brooke stomping on her camera like it was a soda can, it was mega hard to go on with the Jesus-way. But another picture—of Julia tucking the nail file into Brooke's hand and purring instructions—was even clearer.

"We still want to help you," Sophie said.

Brooke shook her head. "Nobody wants to help me. Nobody even likes me."

Sophie felt as if her chest were caving in.

"See?" Brooke said. "You can't say, 'Sure, I like you.'"

No, Sophie thought. *I can't.* Not if she was being her real, honest self.

She swallowed hard. "It's hard to like you because of some of the stuff you do. Only, some of that stuff you sorta can't help because nobody ever helped you with your ADHD—"

Brooke let out a scream that ripped through Sophie. "I don't have that! And I'm not a retard, either!"

She pushed herself away from the wall and, eyes wild, stormed down the hall. Bounding after her, Sophie threw herself onto Brooke's back, and wrapped her arms around her shoulders. She got a face full of red hair.

"Get off me!" Brooke screamed.

"No!" Sophie screamed back—although hers went up into the atmosphere someplace. "Not until you let us help you."

Brooke whipped herself around in the other direction, so that Sophie had to squeeze tight to stay on. There in front of them was Willoughby, standing with her hands on her hips and a cheerleader grin on her face.

"Ready!" she said.

If Sophie hadn't known the plan, she would have thought she was about to do a cheer. She could feel Brooke tighten under her.

"Come on, Brooke," Sophie said into her ear. "Just give us a chance. We'll help you turn yourself in so you won't get into as much trouble, and you can get real help."

"We'll stand by you." Willoughby raised her arms as if she were holding a pair of pom-poms. "We'll be your cheerleaders."

"I hate cheerleaders," Brooke said.

But Sophie felt some of the tightness go out of Brooke's shoulders.

"You don't have to like us," Sophie said. "Just let us help you. That's what Corn Flakes do."

It actually felt good to say it out loud to somebody who wasn't a Corn Flake. And at least Brooke let go a tiny bit more.

"We'll bring Julia and Cassie and Anne-Stuart to you, and you can ask them to tell you the truth about whether they're really your friends," Sophie said.

"And we'll be right there, in hiding," Willoughby said.

"Then you can make your own decision." Sophie hugged Brooke's shoulders. "You're smart enough to do that."

Brooke went so limp, Sophie slid to the floor. Slowly she studied Brooke, and deep inside a question was answered.

After all the Internet research, the Dr. Devon Downing pretending, and the good-girl-Brooke rewards they'd gotten on film, the way to help Brooke was looking right back at her.

Brooke was suddenly a girl that somebody believed in.

Twelve

O kay," Brooke said. "But you can't leave me."

"No way we'll leave you," Willoughby said.

So Brooke trudged behind Willoughby toward the locker hall with Sophie at her side. When they reached the corner, Willoughby pointed to a row of four big garbage cans.

"We'll be right back here, cheering you on," she said.

Brooke sucked at her lip and rounded the corner.

Sophie felt a tap on her shoulder. Kitty motioned for her and Willoughby to duck with her behind the row of trash containers where Maggie was already crouched, notepad and pen in hand. Sophie didn't ask how they'd managed to come up with four honkin' huge garbage cans and drag them there. It was their part of the plan, and they'd done it.

"Did Darbie and Fiona find the Corn Pops?" Sophie whispered to Kitty.

"Some of them," she whispered back. "Fiona's still looking, and Darbie went to get—"

Maggie cut them off by pushing Sophie's head down. Sophie had just hidden behind the middle can when she heard Julia say, "*There* you are. So, do you have my nail file, or what?"

There was silence. Sophie peeked through an opening between garbage cans. She could barely see Brooke nodding.

"She's saying yes," Sophie whispered.

Maggie wrote it down.

"So give it back," Julia said. "And it better not be messed up, or you still have to pay for it."

"And we *know* you can't afford it," Cassie said.

Sophie frowned as her gaze grew focused and very narrow.

"I can't give it back to you right now," Brooke said.

Sophie hoped she wasn't looking back toward the trash cans for cheers. The Pops needed to think this was Brooke's idea.

"I thought you said you had it," Julia said.

"I do—well, I don't ..."

Sophie closed her eyes. *Please, God, let her believe we want to help her. Please let her believe it.*

"She doesn't have it, Julia," Cassie said. "Let's just report that she stole it. Your mom'll buy you another one."

"I didn't steal it!" Brooke said. "You gave it to me, and you told me to use it to mess up Sophie's camera!"

"And you did," Julia said. "And now I want it back."

Sophie didn't have to see her to know that she was holding her hand out like a queen waiting for somebody to kiss it, and that Cassie was ready to do the Corn Pop beheading if Brooke didn't. It had been the crossroads for so many girls before her: Kitty, Willoughby, B.J.

"I'm gonna turn it in with the camera," Brooke said.

"Turn it in to who?" Julia's voice was shrill.

"Whoever Sophie and them tell me to. That way, I won't get in so much trouble."

"Get ready," Willoughby whispered. She grabbed one of Sophie's hands and Kitty grabbed the other. Maggie just kept writing. Sophie wondered if, when Julia attacked Brooke,

Maggie would stay there and get down every last word while the rest of them went into the next phase of the plan.

But there was a sudden quiet down the locker row. Then Julia said, in a voice Sophie had to strain to hear, "Before you turn into a little Corn Flake and go confessing, let's make sure you have your facts straight."

"I do."

"Except the part about the nail file. Do you know whose idea that was?"

"Yours."

"Uh, hel-*lo-o*. No-o-o. I didn't want you taking any kind of risks. It was all Anne-Stuart."

"It was?" Cassie said.

"Shut up, Cassie. You don't know everything Anne-Stuart and I talk about."

During Cassie's stung silence, Julia's voice went even lower. "I hated the idea so much, Brookie, that I will even tell whoever you plan to tell that Anne-Stuart was the one who messed up Sophie's camera, not you. Then you don't even have to mention the nail file, and neither one of *us* will get in trouble."

Sophie heard a loud sniff that couldn't belong to anyone else but Anne-Stuart herself.

"Good job, Fiona," Willoughby whispered.

Sophie saw Maggie make a large check mark on the plan.

"You are *so* not serious, Julia," Anne-Stuart said. "You would actually lie and say I did it, when it was all *your* idea?"

"It was yours, Anne-Stuart," Cassie said.

"Like you so know everything Julia and I talk about, Cassie." Another sniff. "Brooke, Julia's making that up about me so you won't get her in trouble."

"Shut up, Anne-Stuart." It sounded like Julia's teeth were in a vicious clench.

"Don't tell me to shut up."

"Since when do you tell me what to say, Anne-Stuart? I tell *you*—"

"And you know what? I'm sick of it." Anne-Stuart's voice clogged from *not* sniffing. "I've gone along with everything you ever wanted to do to bring down the goody girls—"

"Corn Flakes!" Julia cried. "They're the Corn Flake clique—and if it wasn't for *me*, we never would have found that out. If it wasn't for *me*, they could just go on making everybody think they're all perfect while they take everything away from me that I deserve!"

"Oh, and I didn't help at all," Anne-Stuart said.

"You did what I told you."

"And now you plan to let me take all the blame?" Anne-Stuart's words screeched like a bad microphone. "How could you take *Brooke's* side?"

"Because I need her to keep the Corn Flakes down. So either trust me to get you out of it, or go back to being the loser you were before I found you."

There was a loud smack. Only when Julia gasped did Sophie realize Anne-Stuart had just slapped her. Sophie peered between the trash cans in time to see Anne-Stuart nearly mow Darbie down as she bolted from the scene. Or what Sophie could see of Darbie. She was half hidden by the hulking form of Coach Virile.

"Catfight?" he said.

Sophie couldn't see Julia, Cassie, or Brooke now, but she clearly heard Julia say, "You should go after her, Coach. She destroyed Sophie LaCroix's camera and tried to blame it on poor Brooke."

Sophie could feel her Corn Flakes holding their breath. But she had to believe—

"No, she didn't," Brooke said. "I did it."

"With the nail file she stole from Julia!" Cassie said.

118

"Shut up, Cassie!" Julia said. "Would you just get out of my life!"

It appeared that Cassie did, as fast as she could. Her retreating footsteps echoed down the locker hall.

"I came late to this party," Coach Nanini said, "so excuse me if I'm a little confused."

"Those guys'll tell you," Brooke said. "I did it."

"What guys?"

"Back there."

Sophie rose slowly from behind the trash cans, pulling Willoughby and Kitty with her. Fiona emerged from the opposite bank of lockers. Julia's hair seemed to stop in midtoss, as if the Corn Pop life had just been sucked out of it.

"Anybody want to clear this up for me?" Coach Nanini said. "Little Bit?"

Sophie opened her mouth, but Brooke dodged around Darbie, tripping on her shoelaces in the process. She landed with her face close to Coach's chest. When she looked up at him, Sophie saw tears making trails through the stale makeup, as if they were washing away the last of Project Brooke.

"I did it, and I know it was horrible. I know I'm gonna get in trouble, but I want—" Her mouth snapped shut, and she turned to the Corn Flakes.

"You can do it, Brooke," Willoughby said.

Heads bobbed. Darbie even said, "You won't make a bags of it. Go on then."

Brooke squeezed her eyes tight. "I want help," she said.

"All right," Coach Nanini said. "Let's see if we can't get you some." He looked up at Julia. "Expect to hear from Mr. Bentley first thing tomorrow. This isn't over for you."

Then he walked away with Brooke, head bent toward her like an understanding bear.

119

"I wouldn't believe that just happened if I hadn't seen it with my own eyes," Darbie said.

"We *didn't* see it," Willoughby said. She nudged Kitty. "Nice hiding place."

But Kitty just slipped her hand into Sophie's. "We didn't have to see it to believe it, did we?"

Fiona coughed and nodded down the locker row. Julia was still standing there, staring toward where Anne-Stuart had left, as if she knew she'd reappear any moment to pay the queen her rightful homage. It was either wait there or face the unbelievable truth: Julia'd been abandoned, and without the Pops, she was powerless.

"I wrote down everything they said," Maggie murmured to Sophie.

Sophie shrugged. "We may not actually need it now. I think the Corn Pops are no more."

"What about the Corn *Flakes*?" Kitty said. "Do we still call ourselves that, now that everybody knows?"

They all looked at Sophie.

"I don't think it matters what we're called," she said. "It's all about who we are. That's what counts."

Sophie didn't miss her camera as much as she thought she would. In fact, it was a whole two weeks before she wished she had it. It wasn't to film Brooke telling about her new counselor—Dr. Peter Topping—or Julia becoming so almost-invisible at school that Sophie started praying for her. It definitely wasn't to make a movie about a dream character. None showed up in her mind to try to solve some problem.

No, she decided on a Saturday afternoon when she walked into the family room where Daddy was watching a basketball game with a sleepy baby Hope in his arms. Her tiny sister was the one she wanted to film.

Daddy looked up at Sophie. "I don't think our little rookie cares about the Boston Celtics," he said. "You want to put her in her crib?"

Sophie smiled and put out her arms.

"Way to be a team player, Soph," Daddy said.

Sophie took the steps one by one and placed Hope in her baby bed. She stood looking down at the eyes lightly closed in fairylike sleep. Eyes that were uniquely Hope Celeste LaCroix.

"Maybe my daydreaming days are over," Sophie whispered to her. "I'll always have an imagination—you need one, you know. All Corn Flakes and other authentic people have imaginations—and they're themselves—and they never put anybody down. In fact, they even help people they don't like because they follow the Jesus-way."

Sophie heard her own voice get husky with tears. "I wish you could be a Corn Flake," she whispered. "Maybe I just have to believe God will let you, no matter how different you are."

And then it occurred to her, the truth that—at some level—she'd always known. It made her lean down and kiss her sister's soft forehead.

"I don't have to try to fix you. You are your own unique self. Just like me, and Fiona, and Darbie—"

Hope's eyes fluttered open. She searched Sophie's face as if she were waiting for something.

"Do you want to be a baby Corn Flake?" Sophie whispered.

The little tongue popped out. And then Hope's face brightened into a smile. A wonderful, toothless, knowing smile.

An I-want-to-be-a-Corn-Flake smile.

Sophie smiled back.

And she believed without seeing that Hope would most certainly be one.

Glossary

Attention Deficit Hyperactivity Disorder (uh-TEN-shun DEF-uh-set hy-pur-ak-TIV-eh-tee dis-or-dur) also known as ADHD, it is a brain disorder (or problem with the brain) that makes it hard to pay attention to the right things

the bejeebers (beh-JEE-burs) no one quite knows what bejeebers are, but when someone scares them out of you, it means you feel like your stomach almost jumped out of your body in fright

chromosomes (KROH-muh-zohms) these are super long pieces of DNA that have everything a baby needs to become a human. They decide things like your hair color, or if you're going to be a boy or a girl.

clique (clik) a bunch of friends who don't let anyone else join their group

contraband (KAHN-tra-band) something that is against the rules, and you have to sneak in

defect (DEE-fekt) something that isn't the way it should be

dire (DY-er) horrible, disastrous, and can only lead to bad things

eejit (EE-jit) the way someone from Ireland might say "idiot"

flitters (fli-turs) 1) a feeling you get when you're really excited, like when your body gets all shaky; 2) description of something that's all in pieces

foostering about (foo-stur-ing a-bout) an Irish way of saying "wasting time"

the full shilling (the full SHILL-ing) not all there in the head; acting like your brain cells are missing

genes (jeans) stuff in DNA that your parents pass on to you, which make you who you are. So if you and your mom both giggle the same way, it's because you have her genes.

heinous (HEY-nus) unbelievably mean and cruel

hysteria (hiss-TAYR-ee-uh) crazy and out of control

impulsivity (im-puhl-SIV-eh-tee) always doing things right away instead of thinking about it first; doing things you don't plan on

incense (IN-sents) being really angry

jilted (JILL-ted) describes someone who was suddenly ditched

literally (LIH-ter-uhl-ee) actual fact. So if your homework was eaten by an iguana, it literally happened. Or if you believe something that's meant to be a joke, then you took it too literally or as fact.

make a bags of (mayk a bags of) do a poor job or screw things up

microscope (my-cro-skohp) science equipment that makes very tiny things bigger so that you can see them

mondo (MAHN-doh) another word for "extremely"; describes something that's much bigger or louder than it needs to be

obnoxious (ob-NAWK-shus) really, really annoying

reef (reef) an Irish word that means to beat someone up

remission (re-MIH-shun) when a disease, like cancer, disappears with treatment. If the disease doesn't come back for many years, the person may be cured.

shenanigans (sheh-NAN-eh-gans) playing around and possibly being a little naughty

somber (SAHM-bur) super serious, and not smiling or finding things funny

unrepentant (un-rhee-PEN-tent) not feeling bad about something you did and refusing to apologize

We want to hear from you. Please send your comments
about this book to us in care of zreview@zondervan.com. Thank you.

ZONDERVAN.com/
AUTHORTRACKER
follow your favorite authors

Bibleland Children's Library
Oak Hills Church

9 780310 718451